Formula for PASSION

YAHRAH ST. JOHN

HARLEQUIN®

entertain, enrich, inspire™

Dedicated to Beatrice Astwood for her love and support
and making me feel like a daughter.

Recycling programs
for this product may
not exist in your area.

ISBN-13: 978-0-373-86275-7

FORMULA FOR PASSION

Copyright © 2012 by Yahrah Yisrael

Dear Reader,

Formula for Passion concludes the Adams Affair trilogy with Courtney Adams falling for Jasper Jackson, the son of her family's mortal enemy.

Courtney and Jasper are strangers who embark on a no-strings-attached tryst in the Dominican Republic but soon realize love is on the menu. Life gets complicated when family loyalty seeks to supersede their romance. Expect to see Jasper's father, Andrew Jackson of Jax Cosmetics, take center stage in the drama.

I hope you will find it a satisfying conclusion as I give closure to the Adams and Jackson feud once and for all, while you catch up on your favorite characters: Kayla and Ethan Graham and Shane and Gabrielle Adams.

Visit my website at www.yahrahstjohn.com for the latest updates and details on my next book, expected in spring 2013. Or contact me via email at Yahrah@yahrahstjohn.com.

Warm regards,

Yahrah St. John

A heartfelt thanks to my friends and family for their faith and encouragement. My utmost gratitude to my readers for their continued loyalty. And to Freddie Blackman...for all the love and inspiration.

Chapter 1

"A trip to the Dominican Republic? Sounds fabulous!" Courtney Adams was overjoyed at the prospect of leaving the chilly January weather of Atlanta. As a spokesmodel for Adams Cosmetics, she really did have better perks than her older sister, Kayla, the CEO, and brother, Shane Adams, vice president and head chemist. She'd been in Milan for New Year's Eve for a fashion show, and now no more than two weeks later, she was off to the Caribbean.

"This is not a vacation, Courtney," said her brother-in-law, Ethan Graham, part owner of Adams Cosmetics. "You would be there for Bliss's new campaign." Bliss was the company's third fragrance.

"I'm well aware of that." They'd all been summoned to the conference room for a mandatory board meeting. It was a new-year, new-start sort of thing. "I'm just saying that it's a welcome change after all the drama with Ecstasy's debut." Ecstasy was their previous perfume that, thanks to the machinations of their competitor Jax Cosmetics, had a rocky start in the marketplace. But in the end, Ecstasy's revenues surpassed the knockoff Jax Cosmetics had produced.

"We're looking to capture the clean, modern and oceanic quality to Bliss," Shane added. "And what better way than on the beach? Gabrielle and I—" he smiled over at his fiancée, who'd joined Adams Cosmetics last year "—went there a month ago and we were so impressed that we thought it would be the perfect location for the ad campaign. And once they saw the pictures, Kayla and Ethan agreed."

"Well, I'm there," Courtney responded. "When do I leave?"

"Myra is finalizing your travel arrangements," Kayla said. She'd just finished feeding her five-month-old son, Alexander, and returned from the employee day-care center. "We'd like you to leave by the end of the week."

"You'll love Sea Breeze Resorts," Gabrielle said. "Shane and I found the resort to be first class. The staff is so warm and friendly you'll hate to leave."

"I'm looking forward to it," Courtney replied. She needed a break from all the lovey-dovey in the air. First Kayla and Ethan had gotten married over a year ago and then Shane and Gabby had gotten engaged. And although she'd orchestrated her brother's union, she still felt like the odd man out. Her mother, Elizabeth, was in full mother-hen mode and eager to fix Courtney up with any number of eligible Atlanta bachelors. It was time for her to make like a ghost.

"I'm so excited for this trip," Courtney told Kayla once their meeting adjourned. "I need to get away."

"You have been a little restless these days," Kayla noted. Courtney was usually full speed on all cylinders, but since

Ecstasy's campaign had died down, it had been quiet on the home front. Her little sister had *seemed* content helping plan Shane and Gabrielle's wedding, but Kayla knew better. Courtney craved excitement.

"I've been still for too long," Courtney agreed. "I'm used to having too much to do and now I don't have enough."

"Are you looking for more responsibility in the company?" Kayla inquired.

Courtney nodded. "I can only survive on my looks for so long. I mean, I'm already past my prime in model years. I'm twenty-seven."

"Well, we'd love to have you take a bigger role here. You're not just a pretty face to me. With your marketing degree, you're a real asset to AC."

Courtney smiled broadly. It was nice hearing those words from Kayla. She'd always wanted her big sister's approval, but sometimes that was hard to come by. Kayla had always been very focused on her studies and learning the business, while Courtney had been about having fun and being carefree. It was getting long past time that she started acting like an adult and not an adolescent model.

"Why don't you get whatever *it* is out of your system?" Kayla replied. "And when you get back, be ready to get down to business."

"That sounds like a plan."

"What is going on, Mark?" Jasper Cartwright asked his head of development that same morning in his office at Sea Breeze Resorts in Punta Cana. He'd just reviewed the report from the lender's inspector on his second hotel in the Dominican Republic, Palace at Punta Cana, which was currently under construction, and seen that work wasn't as far along as he'd hoped on the project. To make matters worse, he didn't like the materials the construction company was using. Yet they had passed the bank's inspection. But even if the bank that had lent him the money was satisfied, Jasper wasn't. In his gut he felt something was amiss at the construction site.

"I thought you'd vetted this crew out?" Jasper asked from behind his desk.

"I did," Mark returned. "They were highly recommended by several local businesses."

"And did they use subpar materials on their build-outs too?" Jasper asked testily.

Mark appeared to be offended by Jasper's tone. He'd always taken his job very seriously and clearly didn't like the implication. "You don't know that for sure."

"Don't forget I used to work in construction," Jasper said. "I've done it all, from helping pour concrete to framing the walls to painting. It appears they are using inferior materials from what was drawn on the architectural plans. I want them off the site."

"We can't do that, Jasper. You signed a contract. You would stand to lose millions."

"I've lost faith in this general contractor."

"Then perhaps you should become more involved with the construction from here on out." Over the years, Jasper had allowed Mark to take the lead with this project.

Jasper rubbed his jaw. Mark had a point, and it gave him a crazy idea. Perhaps it was time to get his hands dirty again. Usually he would have been there himself, overseeing things, but he'd had to take a step back when his mother, Abigail, had taken a spill on the steps of her farmhouse in Marietta, Georgia. He'd gone back to the States for a couple of weeks so he could spend some time with her. He'd hired a private nurse to help with her rehabilitation, and she was progressing smoothly.

But now was clearly the time to jump back in. This prime piece of property had fallen into his lap and he couldn't afford to have it wasted because of bad construction. He needed to be more hands-on, and what better way than to go to the construction company and pose as a laborer or better yet a foreman? He could use his background to get hired, which would give him a way of seeing exactly what was going on on-site. Of course, he ran the risk of the general contractor recognizing who he was. But throughout, Mark had been the face of the project, and Jasper had been behind the scenes. He should be able to get by without anyone being the wiser.

"That's exactly what I'm going to do," Jasper stated.

"What makes you tick, Ms. Adams?" the reporter with the *Atlanta Star* asked when he visited the Adams family estate to interview Courtney for the cover of their next magazine. The issue was going to focus on the top thirty under thirty in Atlanta business.

When he'd arrived with a photographer, Courtney had been ready for him. She'd already called ahead to make sure Viola, AC's makeup stylist, was present, because she had to be camera ready and look her absolute best. Her stylist had picked out several different outfits for her to be photographed in. The first was a cream pantsuit with a plunging neckline and the final one was a white, one-shoulder evening gown with a front slit that showed off one toned thigh.

It was increasingly becoming a chore getting all dolled up for the press. As much as Courtney loved the fame, she was ready for a change. The photographer shot Courtney in several areas of the estate, in her bedroom facing her cheval mirror, in the gardens and by the pool. When they were done, they returned to the living room where Victor, their butler, had sweet tea and lemon cake waiting on the coffee table.

"You have it all—fame, wealth and beauty. The world is your oyster. What more could you want?" The reporter set the tape recorder on the coffee table.

"I am pretty lucky," Courtney said, touching her chest. "But let me tell you that fame is fleeting. There will be another pretty face to take my place soon enough."

"I don't know about that," the reporter commented, leaning back against the sofa. "You've dominated the Atlanta scene for over a decade and are always seen in New York, Paris and Milan."

He was right about that. Courtney had loved the spotlight. It was as if she was born to be there, but all good things must come to end. "True, but I guess that dovetails into your other comment. Wealth. I've cultivated my fame to help brand my family's cosmetics company. It's not for personal gain. I'd like to think I've played a part in the company's success."

"I would say so. If you hadn't been in the limelight, no one would know Adams Cosmetics. Which brings me to my next question. For twenty years, Adams Cosmetics was a boutique firm catering to a specific clientele. What has it been like merging with such a corporate Goliath like Graham International?"

Courtney smiled soberly. "It was an adjustment for all of us, but we've acclimated. And now we're bigger and stronger than ever." It had taken a long time for Courtney to feel comfortable with Kayla *and* Ethan running the company. She'd been none too pleased when her brother-in-law had tried replacing her with Noelle Warner, an actress. Who also happened to be his ex-girlfriend. It was doomed from the start. "We've introduced new products in our cosmetics line, revamped our skin-care line and introduced two new fragrances, Hypnotic and Ecstasy. And we have another on the way."

"Sounds like you're a busy lady," he said. "How is your love life faring? I mean with your good looks, men must be bountiful."

Courtney skated by his question and said, "I think I get my good looks from my mother, Elizabeth. She's absolutely stunning."

"Did you inherit those famous green eyes from her?"

"I did. So did my brother."

"That's right, your brother, Shane, is AC's chemist. He's getting married soon, yes?"

"In a couple of months."

"Wow. Your sister and brother both married in the last two years. Does that make you hear wedding bells yourself?"

"Absolutely not." Courtney shook her head fervently. "I love my freedom and am content with the status quo. I'll leave it to my siblings to marry and procreate."

"Are you saying you would never marry?"

Courtney shrugged. "I don't know if I'm the marrying kind. I'm having too much fun being single." And she couldn't wait to hop on a plane and find out just how much fun she could have.

As he drove in an old pickup, Jasper was pleased with himself. In less than an hour, he'd secured a position at Dorchester Construction Company, the company he'd hired to construct his new hotel, and would begin work on Monday. He'd driven his old beat-up Ford pickup truck, because it wasn't as if he could drive his Lamborghini to the hotel site and expect to get hired.

Jasper had acted as if he were a man down on his luck. The superintendent had taken one look at his truck and his attire of ripped jeans and T-shirt and hired him on the spot. It had helped that his foreman had just quit, and he was in need of help. But why would the foreman have quit such an illustrious project? It didn't make sense, and Jasper suspected his gut was right on the money that something was wrong on-site. The superintendent had requested a résumé, which Jasper didn't have, but he'd given him several references, all of whom Jasper phoned in advance to give a heads-up of his plan.

The superintendent had easily fallen for his act. Now Jasper would have the opportunity to finally see what was going on.

When Courtney arrived in Punta Cana on Sunday afternoon after a three-and-a-half-hour flight, she was amazed at just how beautiful the Dominican Republic truly was. Flying over the Atlantic Ocean, she'd gotten a clear view of the island thanks to the cloudless blue sky. She saw sparkling cobalt waters, magnificent palm trees and sandy white beaches. It was Mother Nature at her best.

A hired car greeted her at the airport and whisked her to Sea Breeze Resorts. The hotel was tucked away from the other resorts and required a forty-five-minute drive to get there, but it was worth the wait. Sea Breeze Resorts had its own private beach, plush landscaping and the greenest grass she'd ever seen. Courtney was sure the golf course she'd passed on her way to the main building was a top-ranked course. Golf wasn't her favorite sport, but it was a necessary evil and had gotten her in front of movers and shakers she wouldn't otherwise have met.

The car stopped in front of a whitewashed stucco building, and a bellhop immediately opened the passenger door and helped her out of the vehicle. "Welcome to Sea Breeze Resorts."

"Thank you." Courtney smiled, accepting his hand. She was impressed at the prompt service. Even more so when a man whom she assumed was the hotel manager, dressed in a formal suit, greeted her by name as she walked in the lobby.

"Welcome, Ms. Adams, to Sea Breeze Resorts. My name is Miguel," the older, distinguished gentleman said. "It's a pleasure to have a celebrity of your caliber staying at the resort."

He led her to the check-in desk that was situated in the open-air lobby, where a wood-paneled walkway surrounded two small pools of water lilies and sea turtles. The hotel manager took care of checking her in himself.

"Celebrity? I wouldn't say that." From the lobby, she could see the property's spectacular ocean view and elegant accommodations. The focal point was the seventeenth-century hand-carved wooden archway that encased the entrance and the Dominican art sculptures that adorned the windows.

"But you and your family are featured in this month's *Essence* magazine, are you not?"

Courtney nodded. "Yes, we are." She'd forgotten that Ethan had arranged for the Adams and Graham family to be spotlighted in the magazine.

"Then, you're a celebrity," the hotel manager said. "My name is Miguel and I will be happy to assist you during your stay at Sea Breeze Resorts. We've arranged an excellent suite for you with a majestic view of the ocean from your terrace. You'll love it."

"Thank you so much," Courtney replied. Typically, she was in more cosmopolitan places like New York and Paris. She rarely got to go someplace warm, let alone frolic on the beach. And she intended to do a lot of frolicking on her stay. She'd promised Kayla she would get the wanderlust out of her system, and she intended to do just that.

With all the wedding planning for Gabby, who was inept at fashion, Courtney had been on a self-imposed male hiatus. It was time she had a little fun.

"Allow me to show you to your room and once you've had time to freshen up, I can give you a tour of our fabulous resort."

"That sounds great."

An hour later Courtney had showered in her oceanfront suite. She was duly impressed with the seven-thousand-acre resort and could see why Shane and Gabby had recommended it for the shoot and her stay; it was nothing short of phenomenal. The resort was upscale and infused with modern sophistication and Asian twists in its furnishings and architecture. It was as if the owners had thought of every possible amenity from the infinity-edge pool, the fitness center, the tennis courts to the spa. The manager had indicated there was horseback riding, Jet-Skiing and windsurfing too. It was going to be a great trip, complete with a photo shoot and commercial for Bliss's new campaign.

Thanks to Miguel, she was sat at the chef's table with several other high-profile guests and enjoyed a delicious four-course meal later that evening. Although dinner was incredible, it was three hours long and Courtney was eager to depart and get some rest after flying; tomorrow she would explore the island.

"You've got to be kidding me," Courtney said, pulling her rental car over along the side of the highway. Despite Miguel's insistence that she take a hired car, Courtney had decided to tour the island herself without a guide. She hated to be tethered down to a set itinerary, and she'd had a good time driving around the island all day. But this was not on the menu.

Courtney jumped out of the Dodge Charger in her shorts and tank top and stared down at the rear driver's-side tire. She had a flat. She'd never had a flat in her entire life, and she certainly didn't know how to change one. She glanced around the dirt road but didn't see a car in sight. She'd passed a gas station a couple of miles back, but that was quite a hike. Courtney glanced down at her Manolo Blahnik shoes. They were not made for walking, especially not in ninety-five-degree weather.

It was already sweltering hot outside. The sun was high overhead and Courtney could feel the first beads of sweat beginning to form on her brow. She hated to sweat unless she was playing a sport or being active in her favorite spot: the bedroom. She leaned inside the window she'd rolled down earlier and grabbed the bottled water she'd been smart enough to bring, then took a generous swig.

An hour later, the afternoon sun was baking her delicate café-au-lait skin, so Courtney pulled out the car manual and reviewed how to change a tire. It might as well have been written in Portuguese. She only spoke fluent French and a little Spanish, so she couldn't make heads or tails of it. She would have to fly solo. Courtney opened the trunk and took out the donut from the floor. She found some device called a lug wrench and what she could only assume was a jack to lift the car.

She was bending down to take the lug nuts off the hubcap when she heard the roar of an engine coming down the highway. She had a savior, thank God!

Jasper sighed wearily as he drove back to the resort in his pickup. He'd had a long first day. After completing the usual employment paperwork, he'd met up with the superintendent of the construction company to walk the site. He had put on his hard hat and steel-toe boots and followed him outside. The superintendent had introduced him to his laborers as well as several key subcontractors, such as the electrician, plumber and finisher and painter. Jasper shook hands with each of them. He intended to talk to them extensively, on the sly of course, to see if he could figure out exactly what was going on at his hotel.

The day had been long. Jasper had forgotten what back-breaking work it was to be in construction. He was ready for a nice hot shower and to change into his linen trousers and Tommy Bahama polo shirt. That is, until he saw a statuesque beauty bending down on the side of the road, wearing skimpy shorts and a formfitting tank top.

As he stopped his truck on the opposite side of the road, he got a nice view of her well-shaped behind. He was admiring the view when the beauty gazed up at him. With her hand shielding her face from the sun, she yelled, "If you're done staring at my butt, would you care to lend me a hand?"

Jasper smiled broadly as he jumped out of the vehicle. A woman with attitude! He liked her already. "My, my," he said as he crossed the road, "someone is sure testy."

"You would be too if you'd been standing out in this blistering heat for an hour. I have delicate skin."

"I bet." Jasper chuckled. He was unprepared for the sight that greeted him once he got up close and personal. The woman was tall in what had to be four-inch heels, but that wasn't all. She wasn't just beautiful, she was breathtaking. She had creamy latte-colored skin that complemented her sleek, sophisticated bob with honey-blond highlights. And, well, her green eyes were nothing short of arresting! They stopped him dead in his tracks.

Courtney sighed wearily. She was used to men's reactions toward her looks, but there was something about this one that was a little bit different from the other men she'd encountered. There was something strong about him and his dark chocolate skin that appealed to her on a physical level. She guessed he must be six foot two, maybe three, and despite his less-than-desirable attire of ripped jeans and a T-shirt, he smelled all man.

"Well, are you going to help me or not?" she asked. "Or do you always stare at ladies dumbfounded? I doubt that gets you very far." The second the words were out of her mouth, Courtney realized she sounded a bit harsh.

"Listen, lady." Jasper quickly snapped out of his daze at her tone. "It's you who needs my help, not the other way around." He glanced down at her attempt at changing a flat tire.

Courtney stood up straight. She'd never had someone give it back to her like that, and she had to begrudgingly admire it even if she didn't like it. "You're right, so if you would *please* be so kind as to help me out of a pinch, I would appreciate it."

"That's better!" Jasper walked around the entire length of her rental car and then stated, "Can't do it."

"Well, why the hell not! It's just a flat tire," she responded gruffly.

Jasper laughed at her indignation, which only infuriated Courtney further. She stomped toward him, giving him a great view of her pert bosom in the formfitting tank top. "Because, my dear, you have two flat tires." He inclined his head in the direction of the passenger's-side rear tire.

"How can that be?" Courtney shook her head. "Who gets two flat tires?"

"Apparently you do?" He grinned broadly. "You must have rolled over some nails."

"For Christ's sake!" She should have listened to the

hotel manager instead of going off on her own. Now look where she was, stuck on a dirt road with a construction worker. "Well, if it's money you're after to help me, I'm sure I can accommodate you."

Jasper's eyes narrowed at her condescending tone. This high-class diva was probably used to getting what she wanted with a bat of her eyelashes. She probably thought he was some poor schmuck off the street whom she could speak to any kind of way. She was wrong. "*I* don't have to do a damn thing. And if *I* were you, I wouldn't be throwing around the fact that you have money in these parts. It might attract the wrong sort, if you get my drift." And with that comment, he started walking back toward his truck.

Courtney stormed after him as best she could in four-inch heels on a rocky dirt road. "Wait, just a minute. Where do you think you're going?"

Jasper turned around and Courtney caught a flash of anger in his eyes, but just as quickly it was gone. "I'm leaving. Or do you need me to get an interpreter for you?"

"Oh!" Courtney was flabbergasted. "You're just going to leave me here?"

Jasper opened his truck door and hopped in the driver seat. "That's exactly what I'm going to do. Perhaps you should be more kind to Good Samaritans." He turned on the engine. It sputtered to life and seconds later, he shifted into gear, leaving her staring at his bumper. It was what she deserved considering the way she'd spoken to him. She had acted like a princess and as if she were entitled to a ride. He owed her nothing.

So why did he feel terrible? From his rearview mirror, he could see her standing in the middle of the road. She looked shell-shocked that he had left her stranded on the road in a bad area of town where beautiful, rich women like her disappeared in a nanosecond.

Seconds later, Jasper was reversing his truck to scoop her up. His mother had raised a gentleman, so he couldn't very well leave her alone. When he reached her, her arms were folded across her chest and he could see she was pouting. He swung open the passenger door. "Get in!"

Courtney paused, debating whether she should get in the vehicle. It was dirty and looked as though he hauled debris of some sort in it. Not to mention the fact that he could be some crazy ax murderer. How would she know? She probably wouldn't realize it until he'd taken her to some abandoned house in the woods never to be heard from again.

"I'm not going to ask you a second time, princess," Jasper warned.

Courtney didn't have a whole lot of options. If she stayed there, she could be stuck until nightfall and what would become of her? Throwing caution to the wind, she jumped inside the truck. Something in her gut told her she could trust him. Plus, she didn't want to be left on the dirt road to fend for herself. She would just have the hotel manager send someone for the car.

"I am not a princess," Courtney said, looking over to hazard a glance at the stranger.

"You sure act like one," Jasper replied, shifting into gear and pulling back onto the highway.

"Wow, you sure know how to talk to a lady."

"Is that what I'm doing? I thought I was giving you a ride back to your resort. Because trust me, if I was trying to *talk* to you, you would know it."

Courtney turned around and stared at the stranger. She was surprised, but yet oddly turned on by his confidence. He didn't seem to have the same social graces that some of her boy toys did, but perhaps that was why she tired of them so easily. "You sure are cocky."

"I've been told that before."

"But you don't care?"

Jasper shrugged, which Courtney took to mean he couldn't care less what others thought about him. She wished she could do the same. She always had to be conscious of how she was viewed by the public. It was up to her to sell the Adams Cosmetics brand, so her every movement was calculated. She supposed it was why when she was eighteen, she had done something completely reckless.

She'd gotten married to Chaise Anderson, whom she'd known only a few weeks. She'd met Chaise, the son of a wealthy Atlanta businessman, at a local party. He was good-looking, charming and sexy. The attraction between them had been instant. So when Chaise suggested they run away to Vegas to get married, Courtney had been on board. She'd been dying to get out of her parents' grip, and marriage had seemed like the next best thing. The marriage hadn't lasted longer than a few days because, as soon as her father, Byron, had found out, he'd flown to Vegas. She'd gotten quite the tongue-lashing about the image she was portraying and he'd insisted she have the marriage annulled. Courtney had never seen her father so furious and she had quickly agreed. But truth be told, she'd liked being free and reckless, if only for a little bit.

The remainder of the drive continued in silence with the exception of Courtney asking the stranger to roll up the window and turn on the air-conditioning. That's when he'd promptly informed her there was no a/c and they hadn't spoken a word since. Clearly, her handsome stranger was a man of few words.

He also looked like the type who knew how to handle a woman in the bedroom. Where had that thought come from? She didn't mind a bad boy every now and then, but they were usually the clean-cut type, trust-fund babies who liked to have fun. But this guy, he was different from the men she usually encountered. There was something a little dangerous about him and it was kind of a rush. Courtney shook her head, trying to shake the thought out of her head, but she was having a hard time focusing. They were in such close quarters she could smell his woodsy earth scent, and it was making her horny.

She was happy when the resort finally came into view and the truck made an unceremonious stop in front of the entrance. She turned to the stranger at her side and said, "Thanks for the ride." She reached inside her purse for her wallet, but the stranger placed his large dark hand over hers. Courtney felt a tingle shoot straight from her hand to her core.

"Think I told you about offering folks money," he said. "Didn't I?"

Courtney lowered her eyes and blushed. "You did. So perhaps I can buy you a drink as a thank-you?" She looked up at him and a smile spread across her lips.

When Jasper's dark eyes stared into her green ones, Courtney swallowed hard. Her throat felt parched and she licked her lips. The stranger's eyes followed her movement, and that made her nervous. Why was he so silent? *Speak, for goodness' sake!*

Jasper thought about the princess's offer. Despite her efforts to appear aloof, he could see she was attracted to him. Her body language was giving it away, and he noticed her breasts in the tank top perk up at his long gaze. And then wetting those full, sumptuous peach-stained lips told him everything he needed to know. Normally, he would accept and take what she was offering, but he had a feeling the princess was used to getting what she wanted, so he would decline right now. And then have fun making her work for it.

"I have a couple of errands to run," Jasper replied. "But maybe later?"

She frowned. "Fine." She threw her purse over her shoulder, opened the truck door and climbed out. "Thanks again for the ride," she said over her shoulder without hazarding another glance at him.

"'Bye, princess." Jasper waved.

She stomped inside the resort and didn't see the hotel manager come out to greet Jasper.

"Would you like me to put the truck away for you, sir?" Miguel asked Jasper when he came around to the driver's side.

"That's not necessary. I'm heading to my villa." Jasper watched as Courtney's rear disappeared from his view. His villa was located on the outskirts of the Sea Breeze Resorts property. It was close enough for him to check on the resort, but far enough away for him to have his privacy.

"She's breathtaking, isn't she?"

"So you noticed, Miguel? I thought you didn't look at patrons."

"I usually don't, sir, but she's hard not to notice, yes?"

Jasper leaned out over the window and patted the man's back. "I agree, wholeheartedly. So, what do you know about the lady? Who is she?"

"If you come into my office, sir," Miguel said, "I can fill you in on the details."

Chapter 2

Courtney couldn't believe the man had turned her down. She'd hoped for a quick drink, or maybe even a long roll in the hay with her construction worker. He looked as though he had lots of stamina. Unfortunately, she was left to comb the resort for some fun on her own.

After a long, hot shower and a massage and facial at the resort spa, Courtney was ready for the evening. After a spritz of Bliss over her body, she slid on a long maxi dress in a bold Copacabana print and some ornament-encrusted thong sandals and headed to the bar.

As she entered, Courtney noticed that every male eye in the room turned to her. She wasn't unaware that the halter maxi dress plunged at the neckline to show off her pert breasts or that the dress plunged to her waist to show her bare back.

The bar was pretty busy and the band had already started playing some merengue music. Courtney scanned the bar looking for an opening and got more than she bargained for when a pair of dark eyes focused solely on her. *He* was here. How many dark-chocolate, six-foot-three brothers, with a killer smile that could make your panties wet, were on the island? Courtney's breath caught in her throat. He'd changed his mind, but why? He'd seemed determined to make her feel like a fool for asking him out, so she would give it back to him and act as if she didn't recognize him.

Courtney sauntered to the bar and sat across the way from her stranger. *He* could come to her. She knew it was a dangerous cat-and-mouse game they were playing, but she was secretly thrilled at the prospect. She needed a spark of excitement in her life after watching her brother and sister fall in love.

She didn't have time to order a drink because, shortly after being seated, one of the men who'd been openly staring at her approached.

From across the room, Jasper drank his Presidente and watched the beautiful seductress through dark lashes. She'd seen him and knew he was here, but she had been content to sweep past him and go to the opposite end of the bar. But from here he could watch her every move. And watch he did.

He watched the gentle sway of her hips as she walked. He watched the breeze as it blew through her short bob. And he was far from oblivious of the swarm of men who had encircled her. She was holding court like the Queen of England, smiling at one, lightly touching another's arm as she spoke and batting her eyelashes at another. She was an incorrigible flirt!

Miguel had filled him in on all the details about Courtney Adams. She was the illustrious spokesmodel for

Adams Cosmetics. Courtney came from money and was probably used to fame and the power it could bring. According to Miguel, she'd used it to keep her family's company in the public eye. He'd bet she flirted with every man she came into contact with. She probably couldn't help herself.

The company she worked for, Adams Cosmetics, sounded oddly familiar. He searched far back into his memory, digging for the name. Finally it hit him. Adams Cosmetics was the very same company that his father, Andrew Jackson, had always competed against. Jasper had gotten away from all the madness, but now he'd stumbled right into the lion's den by meeting his father's rivals' daughter.

But that didn't stop him from being annoyed at the prospect of other men surrounding a woman he felt he had already laid claim to. Of course, she didn't know that. He'd been aloof when he'd declined her invitation to spend the evening together, but it was time he corrected the matter and got down to business.

"What do you have, pretty lady?" The bartender had finally come around to her side of the bar.

"She'll have a Presidente," a masculine voice said from behind her. "What I'm having."

Courtney's heart turned over in her chest. He had come over. She spun around on her barstool to face him. He was so close to her she could smell the strong woodsy scent of his cologne wafting to her nose. Jasper had used intimidation to push the other men away to get to her side. All her suitors had taken several steps back and were watching them wearily.

"Excuse me, what do you think you're doing?" Courtney finally found her voice and eyed him up and down.

He looked casually fine in relaxed jeans and a black shirt open at the collar.

"Getting your attention," Jasper responded. After a cold shower at his villa had been unable to alleviate the hard-on the honey blonde had caused him, he'd returned to his resort to see if she would deliver on the promise that had been in those dazzling green eyes of hers.

Courtney couldn't help smiling—he was completely arrogant and she dug it. "Well, you have it," she said, and motioned to the seat beside her.

Jasper slid onto the barstool next to hers.

"I thought you were too busy with *errands* to join me."

"I finished up early."

"And decided to grace me with your presence? How generous of you."

"I figured I couldn't allow a woman as beautiful and sexy as you to sit alone at a resort bar," Jasper replied smoothly. "The vultures would be circling." He eyed the rest of the men at the bar who were giving him the evil eye.

"So you think I'm sexy?"

Jasper eyed her up and down. "In that dress, hell yeah." He laughed. "But then again, you were pretty hot in those skimpy shorts and top earlier."

She gave him a sideways glance. "I thought you hadn't noticed."

"I'd be dead not to." Jasper sipped on his beer.

"So we've established that you find me attractive," Courtney replied, and spun around to face him. The chemistry between them was palpable. She was sure everyone else had to feel their sizzling connection. "So what now?"

There was a lot of innuendo behind Courtney's remark, but Jasper opted to be good, for now. "How about we start with names? Mine's Jasper. And yours?"

"Courtney."

Jasper held up his drink. "To having a good time."

"To a good time." Courtney clinked her glass against his.

Courtney didn't remember how many drinks she had because Jasper had been regaling her with tales of his life in construction and all the mishaps he'd had. Although he hadn't said as much, she figured he was a construction worker. He appeared to love what he did for a living. Courtney didn't say much about her job, only that she was in public relations for her family's company. Jasper seemed happy with that. Neither one of them had offered much in the way of personal information. They were just having a good time.

They did shots of Patrón and then got up to dance. Jasper grasped her hand and they made their way into the throng that had congregated on the dance floor and danced to the merengue band. He was an excellent dancer and easily guided Courtney across the floor. And once his hands were on her body, there was no denying the attraction coursing between the two of them. At the touch of his hands caressing her bare back, a fire spread through Courtney's loins. *Does he feel it too?*

When Courtney's pert breasts grazed against his chest, she felt his lower half respond. And when she ground herself against his arousal to the beat of the music, he groaned and she thought he would lose it and take her right there on the dance floor. But he didn't. He must have wanted the moment to last longer, because he slowed the pace, and it allowed her to feel the delicious friction of their bodies meeting.

They continued dancing and drinking until the wee hours of the morning when Jasper pulled her aside.

"Wanna get out of here?" he murmured against her ear as he flicked his tongue lightly across it.

Courtney shivered and said, "Yes."

When they left the bar, the crowd had already thinned out and retired for the night. They walked barefoot toward the beach, since Courtney had abandoned her high heels earlier in the night. That's when Jasper whisked Courtney into the nearby gazebo. It was dark and granted them plenty of coverage so Jasper could kiss her. His movements were slow and methodical. He snaked his arm around her waist and pulled her firmly to him. Courtney's head fell back in response because she knew what was coming next. That deliciously sinful mouth of his on hers. He didn't disappoint. He kissed her the way a soldier kissed the first woman he saw after coming home from a long war.

It was dangerous and passionate, thrilling and exhilarating, all at the same time. His tongue traced the outline of her lips, eager to be inside her warm, waiting mouth. Courtney allowed him entry. His tongue delved into the deep recesses of her mouth and he stroked her tongue with his before sucking hers. Courtney wound her arms around Jasper's neck and kissed him back with equal fervor. His firm chest pressed against her, causing a tight ache to form in her breasts.

Jasper's hands palmed her backside, pulling her closer to him. There was no mistaking it, Jasper was as turned on as she was. Courtney reveled in the fact that she could make her tall, dark stranger feel the way she did, because she'd been burning up since the moment she saw him.

"I want you now," Jasper groaned as his tongue traced her ear with light flicks.

"Oh, yes." Courtney shuddered. "I want you too."

Jasper knew exactly how to tease her earlobe to send her mind swirling and make her dizzy and light-headed. She sighed, tingling with anticipation of what she knew was to come, but Jasper suddenly pulled away.

"Wait here. Be right back." And he was gone in a flash.

After the heat of his skin left hers, Courtney felt bereft. She looked around her and it was dark, with only a faint glow from the stars overhead. Just when she thought he'd abandoned her, Jasper returned with a blanket and laid it across the floor of the gazebo.

Before she could think about what they were about to do out in the open, Jasper was pulling her down on the blanket. It was surprisingly thick and soft against her knees.

Jasper noticed that Courtney's eyes lowered slightly and she pulled away. "Haven't you ever done it outside before?"

Her pupils dilated and Courtney blushed, which thankfully he couldn't see in the dark. She didn't want him to think she was a prude. "Well, no, but I guess there's a first time for everything." She'd always been a little bit of an exhibitionist, but what if someone saw them? She glanced around the dark night.

"Are you afraid to?" he asked, stroking her cheek lightly. "Because we're far away enough that no one can see us."

"You sure do know a lot about this place," Courtney said. "Do you do this often? You know, pick up American women and take them to bed?" How else could he have procured a chenille blanket in the middle of the night?

Jasper paused. "Actually I don't, but since the moment I saw you—" he crawled toward her on his hands and knees "—I wanted to kiss you, to taste you." He slid his hand around her neck, leaned his head to one side and laid claim to her lips.

He lifted his head slightly so Courtney could regain her breath and said, "Now's your chance, princess, to back out, because once we get started I can't promise I'll be able to stop."

"Who said I would want you to?"

They reached for each other at the same time and tumbled down onto the blanket. It was a long, drugging kiss that sapped Courtney of all rational thought. Warning bells were ringing that she shouldn't be outside making love with a stranger underneath the stars, but she didn't care. She gave in to the emotion and...it was sweet heaven.

Jasper's well-defined mouth took full possession of hers. It started when his warm and moist tongue played with the outer corners of her mouth before darting inside for a taste. Then his tongue thrust deeper, penetrating the hollows of her mouth. He made love to her mouth and she shivered with desire.

He pulled back slightly to rain kisses across her forehead, her eyelids, her cheeks and then back to pay tribute to her lips. He grappled with the halter at her nape until he was finally able to release the knot and free her breasts to his searing gaze.

Jasper found Courtney's breasts to be high and round and ready for him. The tips of his fingers reached out to glide their way down her satin skin before his mouth came down on them, hot and rampant. He took one nipple between his teeth and lightly sucked on it, tormenting her. He drew circles around the bud with his tongue and drew her into his mouth. He loved the other breast with equal measure. She clasped his head to her breasts, never wanting him to stop, but Jasper was clearly eager for more.

"Now, Jasper."

"Not yet."

He ignored her pleas and continued his quest by caressing her shoulders, then her bare back, then lowered to the contours of her hips, one inch at a time. A ribbon of desire coiled through Courtney, so she didn't object when he slid her maxi dress higher and higher until it was at her waist and he could slip his hand between her thighs and cup her intimately.

There were no second thoughts because she was warm and welcomed his hand. And when he rotated his palm across her mound and pushed the tiny fabric that was her thong aside, Courtney let out a whimper of consent.

He slid his fingers between her damp folds and began rubbing light circles around the nub. He watched Courtney's eyes dilate as she struggled for control. His thumb continued stroking. She was flushed and he could feel the heat coming off her in droves. Oh, yes...she was oh so damp down there. He thrust his finger farther inside her until she began to tremble.

"Yes! Yes!" *Oh, dear God.* The man had a way with his hands.

"Yes, baby." The urge to bury himself inside her was overwhelming, but he wanted her to come. He wanted to see the look on her face when she did, to know that she enjoyed his ministrations. He could only imagine how good it would feel once he was inside her. He thrust his tongue deep inside her mouth, kissing her feverishly, all the while his fingers delved deeper and deeper inside her. Only when her inner muscles clenched around him and she screamed out his name did he finally relent.

"Are you ready for me, baby?" Jasper nuzzled her neck and ear.

Courtney answered him by grappling with his belt buckle and zipper. "We need a condom."

Jasper helped her by pulling his pants and briefs to his ankles and removing a condom from his pocket, while Courtney discarded her thong.

"Did you know this was going to happen?" she asked, looking up at him as he sheathed himself.

Jasper grinned mischievously. "I only hoped."

One hard, muscular thigh moved between her legs to spread her wide, and the erection she'd felt all night as they danced was now pressed against the opening of her womanhood. She welcomed it. He worked his hardness back and forth over her aroused flesh, causing delicious sensations to whirl through Courtney from the crown of her head to the tips of her toes.

"Now!" Courtney urged. She was teetering on the edge and she needed him inside her. He nudged the tip inside, slow at first, and then he sank into her in one slow, powerful glide. Courtney felt every hot, hard and powerful inch of him. When he was sure her inner muscles had stretched to receive him, Jasper began withdrawing and reentering at a steady rhythm, going deeper and deeper. And as he stroked he covered her body, breasts and lips with hot, desperate kisses. He muttered short phrases. "Courtney! You feel. So wet. And. So good."

She urged him on by rocking her hips. The impact caused her to reach another shattering orgasm. "Jasper!" she cried, lifting the top half of her body and clutching him to her. A moment later, she shattered as tremors racked her body.

His tempo increased and she felt him reach his climax seconds after hers. He shuddered against her and fell atop her, then withdrew and rolled to his side.

They were both looking up at the ceiling of the gazebo. "Wow!" Jasper murmured as he pulled her closer in the darkness. "That was incredible. You're amazing, Courtney."

"You weren't too bad yourself." She was in awe of what they had just shared. Courtney stretched languidly, and her last thought was that Jasper might be dangerous to her well-being.

Chapter 3

The next morning, Courtney was startled to find herself naked in a king-size bed with a muscled arm across her naked body. Whose room was this?

The last thing she remembered was drinking shots of Patrón, dancing all night long and making love with Jasper in the gazebo outside. What had gotten into her? She'd thought she'd stopped being so reckless after her two-day marriage to Chaise. Sure, she liked her freedom and this had been wonderful, but it had also been utterly stupid. Anyone could have seen her out there and taken photos and sent them to the press! She was supposed to be the image of Adams Cosmetics. She'd come down here on business, so how would her family feel if she'd been caught in flagrante delicto?

Well, what was done was done, and she had to move forward. Somehow she had to extricate herself from the situation as gently as possible. Courtney tried to rise from the bed, but that only prompted Jasper to stir beside her.

"Good morning, sunshine," Jasper said as Courtney turned over to face him.

"Morning," she replied, stifling a yawn with the back of her hand. "I assume you carried me back here?"

Jasper nodded. "I believe I wore you out last night," he said as he stretched. When he moved, the sheets moved with him and revealed a long expanse of hairless, muscled chest. A vivid memory of running her hands across it came to mind.

"Likewise, it was a very enjoyable evening." And she had the sore muscles to prove it. "But how can you afford this place?" She motioned around the room as she sat up, clutching the sheet to her bosom.

Jasper shrugged, watching her feeble attempt to cover herself up. He'd seen, tasted and touched everything she had. "I know a few people at the resort that owe me some favors." He kind of liked the fact that Courtney thought him some poor slob who couldn't afford an expensive room like this. Perhaps he would get a chance to see the real Courtney.

"Well, aren't you the man?" Courtney said, smiling as she threw the covers back. "I have a busy day ahead, so I'm going to get going." She made a move to leave, but Jasper pulled her down until she was flat on her back. He didn't allow her to utter another word. Instead, his large hands took her face and held it gently. He stared at her for several long moments before he planted a tantalizing kiss on her, coaxing a response from her. She kissed him back, lingering and savoring each moment.

When he finally lifted his head, Courtney was out of breath. "Wow" was all she could mutter. Her memory of last night was somewhat fuzzy, thanks to the liquor, but she was fully awake and alert now, and Jasper was an excellent kisser.

"Did you think I would let you go that easily?" Jasper asked, moving from her lips to nibble and lick on her ear. He'd been immediately attracted to her spunk and her vitality and wasn't ready for that to end. Courtney wiggled underneath him, trying to move away, but Jasper pulled her into his arms until she was above him. He circled one hand around her neck and pulled those rosy lips of hers back on his.

"That was not supposed to happen," Courtney said afterward, falling back on the pillows. She couldn't move because she was completely depleted. Jasper wasn't just an excellent kisser; he was also a good lover. He was very giving and ensured that she was thoroughly satisfied before his own needs were fulfilled. He'd immediately squelched her feeble protests of leaving with one kiss. Then he'd made love to her until she had no thoughts of leaving his bed.

"You thought you'd make a quick exit and take the walk of shame back to your room, didn't you?" he asked, turning around to face her with his head resting on his chin.

Courtney couldn't resist laughing at Jasper's bluntness. "Uh…something like that."

"Well, I'm not going to make it that easy for you, Courtney," Jasper said evenly. "I think you and I both know how combustible our union was just now and how hard that is to come by."

Jasper was right. Courtney couldn't recall her climaxes being quite that explosive before, and if the shout that Jasper gave as he came was any indication, it had been the same for him. But so what? What else did they have in common outside the bedroom?

"I can read what's going on in your mind," Jasper said, interrupting her thoughts.

She raised an eyebrow. "Oh yeah? And what was I thinking?"

"You were thinking that we have nothing in common other than great sex. So I'm going to offer you a proposition. Stay with me on Punta Cana and find out. No strings attached. And at the end of your trip, we both go our separate ways." It had been a long time since someone had intrigued him like Courtney, and he wasn't ready for that to end just yet.

"You want me to stay here in a no-strings-attached fling?" Courtney asked. "Wow, you do think highly of yourself."

"Don't act like it's just me," Jasper said. "I know you felt it too. We have a connection of sorts, and I'm just saying we should enjoy it for as long as you're here. Why should we deprive ourselves?" He dazzled her with his perfect white smile.

Courtney stared at Jasper. Here was her fantasy man live in the flesh. Should she go for it? Then her mind came back to Ethan's comment that she was there for work. But then again, she had said she would have fun on this trip, and Jasper was offering her exactly what she *said* she wanted.

"I need to think about it." Courtney slid off the bed and headed toward the bathroom but stopped in her tracks. "Of course, if you want to join me in the shower to try and convince me otherwise, I wouldn't be opposed to it."

"Absolutely!" Jasper hopped off the bed and followed her into the bathroom.

Hours later, once Courtney had returned to her hotel room, she decided to call her best friend, Tea. They'd met seven years ago when Adams Cosmetics had hired Tea's public-relations firm for one of Courtney's earlier campaigns for Adams Cosmetics. The two women had hit it off instantly and been friends ever since. Because Tea was a couple of years older than Courtney, she helped keep Courtney grounded whenever she got the itch to do something crazy.

Courtney had always wondered where she got her wanderlusting free spirit from. Her father and Kayla were hotheaded workaholics devoted to Adams Cosmetics, while Shane and her mother were more cerebral and creative. Shane had been developing products for AC since he was twenty-five, and their mother was a talented artist. Some of her artwork had been featured in AC campaigns.

Although Courtney loved her family and shared a bond with each of her siblings, she always considered herself somewhat of a rebel. She hated to conform, but that was exactly what had happened when she'd agreed to be AC's spokesmodel ten years ago. Little did she know how much freedom she would be giving up, but now Jasper was offering her a taste of living on the edge. It secretly thrilled Courtney, but she needed some advice. What better person than her BFF, Tea?

Courtney glanced at her watch from her hotel-room terrace, and then used her iPhone to dial Tea's work number in Atlanta.

"Tea Santiago."

"Tea, it's Courtney." Courtney slid open the glass doors and sat on one of the terrace lounge chairs, facing the Atlantic. The day was warm, and Courtney was soaking in some of the fresh air and cool ocean breeze.

"Hey, girlfriend, how's DR treating you?" Tea asked.

"Tea…DR is treating a sista real good."

"Oh yeah? Did you get yourself some last night? I know you said you were long overdue."

How was it that Tea could read her so well if they were an ocean apart? "The sex was spectacular!"

"Wow! Spectacular, huh? I've had good sex before, even great, but never spectacular."

"My point exactly," Courtney said. "Which is why I'm considering having myself an island fling with a construction worker. Jasper is his name. Doesn't his name just sound sexy? Anyway, he propositioned me to prolong our one-night stand into a fling for the duration of my trip."

"I thought you only needed to stay for a few days for the campaign."

"True, but I'm long overdue for a vacation, so perhaps I'll extend my trip and stay awhile."

"This Jasper must have done some number on you," Tea said, "because you have never stuck around long enough with any man for him to make an impact."

"Ouch."

"I don't mean it harshly, Courtney. You know I love you. But you don't do commitments. You never have. In your personal life, you're all about fun and freedom. I think it's because you don't have that flexibility in your career."

Courtney was silent on the other end. She knew Tea was right, but to hear her private thoughts out there in the open, to have her best friend shine a light on them, was disconcerting.

"Are you still there?" Tea asked. "Did I say too much?"

"No," Courtney finally said. "You're not saying anything I haven't thought before. But it does make me wonder if I'm capable of something more."

"Professionally or personally?"

"Both. I mentioned to Kayla before I left that I wanted a larger role in Adams Cosmetics, other than being the face of the company."

"I'm so glad to hear you say that," Tea said. She'd been

waiting for her friend to speak up and step out of her older sister and brother's shadow at AC. "You're capable of a lot more, Courtney. I think your family still thinks of you as the baby and the free spirit. In the meantime, enjoy this Jasper. Get him out of your system and then come back to Atlanta and show your family what you're made of."

Even though they were a thousand miles apart, Courtney smiled at her best friend. "That's why I love you, Tea, because you always give me sound advice. So I'm going to have my fun with Jasper now. You know, love 'em and leave 'em. Then come back ready for bear."

"Have fun and be safe," Tea said. "And please do everything I wouldn't do."

"Count on it."

"So, where have you been?" Mark asked Jasper, when he returned to the office the following afternoon. He'd been shocked when the morning passed and Jasper hadn't come to work. It was now 1:00 p.m.

"Getting myself hired at Dorchester's construction company," Jasper replied.

"So he fell for the bait?"

"Yeah, that old pickup truck really did the trick."

"So what now?"

"Well, I'll work there for a few weeks and see exactly what his operations are and find out how he's constructing my hotel."

"You're actually going to do manual labor?"

Jasper laughed. He didn't take Mark's comment as an insult. It had been a while since he'd been hands-on. "I'm not above manual labor. How else do you think I started Sea Breeze Resorts? I had to get my hands dirty."

"I know, but you don't like to talk about your past much." Not many people knew his true identity. That Jasper Jackson was the son of millionaire Andrew Jackson. He'd always kept a low profile, staying out of the public eye to ensure no one made the connection. He never did interviews and was considered somewhat of a recluse. Jasper had confided in Mark, his right-hand man, years ago, but he'd sworn him to secrecy. So Mark had never told another soul.

"That's because there's not much to speak of."

Mark regarded him questioningly. "I know there's more to the story, but I'm going to leave you be. I have a conference call to get to. Let me know how your investigation goes and if you need my help."

"Will do," Jasper said as Mark left his office. When he was gone, Jasper rose from his chair and gazed out the window.

Mark was right that he didn't like talking about his past. Jasper had made a point of distancing himself from his immoral, ruthless father and never looked back. Andrew Jackson was a calculating bastard who cared more about his money than his family. When he'd met Jasper's mother, Abigail, she was a country girl from Marietta, Georgia. She had no idea about the likes of a slick, city boy like Andrew. One night, she made the fateful mistake of meeting Andrew after he'd learned that his true love, Elizabeth, was marrying Byron Adams. He'd seduced Abigail that night as a consolation prize. Unfortunately for Andrew, his mother had ended up pregnant.

Jasper doubted he would have married his mother back then if she hadn't been carrying a son, an heir to the Jackson family fortune. He married Abigail to ensure that his son was legitimate, but he didn't love her and his mother knew it. She hated every minute of life at the Jackson Manor. Initially, she'd tried to be a good wife in the hopes that Andrew would fall in love with her, but that had never happened. She'd even tried to have more children, but two miscarriages later, the doctor had told her to stop trying. That's when she knew her marriage was over and went running back to her family farm. She'd tried to take Jasper with her, but Andrew had steadfastly refused. "My son will stay with me," he'd insisted, vowing to fight her in court if she dared try to keep him away from his son.

And so Jasper had stayed in that cold mausoleum of a house at seven years of age, missing his mother, whom he was only able to see on the odd day Andrew was in a good mood and allowed a visit. Andrew had retained full custody with minimal visitation rights to his mother because he'd bought the bank that held the mortgage to his grandfather's farm, which was in debt at the time. He'd threatened to foreclose on the farm if Abigail didn't give Andrew full custody. So she didn't fight for custody, and in return, Andrew paid off the mortgage on Jasper's grandfather's farm. But as soon as Jasper had turned fifteen, he'd petitioned the court to become an emancipated minor.

Andrew had been livid and had intended to fight Jasper every way until Jasper indicated he knew a lot more about the company's business practices than Andrew wanted the world to know. He'd blackmailed his own father, but it had freed him to move in with his mother at the farm. She was overjoyed, since she always blamed herself that she hadn't been able to keep him. Jasper had understood. Andrew had all the Jackson money behind him.

Jasper had loved living on the Cartwright farm with his mother, grandfather and uncle Duke and his family. His grandfather had shown him everything about farming while his uncle Duke had taught him construction from the ground up. After college, when Jasper was ready to strike out on his own, he'd changed his name. He wanted no relation to Andrew. He'd received a small business loan, and the rest was history.

For thirty-three years old, he'd accomplished a lot. He already had a small chain of boutique hotels, with one in Florida and now his second in the Dominican Republic. He was proud of his accomplishments and that he'd done it all without a dime from Andrew. He'd never been able to call the man his father because he'd despised him for keeping his mother from him. He hadn't spoken a word to him since he'd walked out at fifteen.

Jasper heard Andrew had eventually remarried—a woman named Blythe who had a daughter named Monica. Rumor had it that his stepdaughter was a chip off the old block and had Andrew's killer instinct. *More power to her, because I want no part of Andrew Jackson's legacy.*

Jasper was happy when his cell phone rang, knocking him out of his reverie. He didn't like strolling down memory lane. It always left a bad taste in his mouth. He smiled when he heard the voice on the other end. It was Courtney.

"Hello, gorgeous. Have you given any more thought to my proposition?"

"I have."

"And? Don't leave me in suspense." *Please say yes, please say yes.* He couldn't remember the last time he'd had so much fun, talking and dancing and making love. He was clearly working too hard, and Courtney Adams was just the medicine he needed to cure him of being a workaholic.

"I say yes," Courtney replied. "What are you doing this evening?"

"Spending time with you." He was excited about another night in the seductive temptress's arms.

"Should I come to you this time?" Courtney asked.

"Oh, no," Jasper replied, a little too quickly for his liking. "I can come to the resort."

"Are you sure? This pampered princess doesn't have a problem slumming it," she joked, using the nickname he'd given her.

"It's no problem. I wouldn't dream of taking you away from your creature comforts." He was one to talk, considering he was in a lavish custom-designed office. Yet he wasn't ready to reveal himself to Courtney just yet. He was finally having some long-overdue and much-needed fun. There was no reason that Courtney should find out he was related to Andrew, especially since they'd both agreed to use first names only. Plus, he'd had no connection with the man in nearly twenty years.

"All right, I'll meet you at sunset, Room 4410," Courtney added. "And be ready to show me Punta Cana's nightlife."

"I'll see you then." Jasper hung up. He was sure Courtney was used to dating rich playboys all the time and was probably bored to tears of the same ol' same ol'. It was probably a refreshing surprise to have some fun with a hardworking chap like him. He told himself this charade was all for her benefit, but it was partly for him too. He'd been engrossed in work for far too long and needed to start enjoying life while he was still in his prime. Courtney Adams was just the outlet.

Yes, he knew who she was, heiress and spokesmodel for Adams Cosmetics. Yet she knew nothing about him and for now he was fine with keeping up the pretense. After they'd had their fun, Courtney would tire of him and be back on a plane to the U.S.

Chapter 4

Courtney had never been nervous about dressing for a man before, but oddly enough she was for Jasper. She wanted to entice him, but she also didn't want to flaunt her wealth either. She decided on a casual, wine-colored strapless jumpsuit with a wide-legged pant. She dressed it up by adding a dangling gold necklace and a pair of sexy heeled sandals. She didn't wear much makeup, as the tropical temperature wasn't conducive to a fully made-up face. A touch of mascara and one glide of sparkling lip gloss and she was ready for the night.

Jasper arrived promptly at her suite door at 7:00 p.m.

He looked as dreamy as ever. His dark skin glistened from the crisp white shirt he wore casually opened at the nape, which he'd paired with a pair of well-worn jeans that did justice to his powerful build. But it was the sexy goatee over the full lips that she remembered, and it was why she went directly toward him. Courtney didn't know why she was being so bold, but she'd had a burning desire, an aching need, to be kissed by him again.

She grasped Jasper by his shirt collar and touched her lips softly against his. He took the invitation and circled his arms around her waist and walked her backward inside the room and used his foot to shut the door behind him. His tongue parted her lips and hungrily caressed her while his hands smoothed their way down her backside. Courtney moaned and moved her hips provocatively against him.

It was divine ecstasy when he kissed her, and the flame that had been swelling inside her turned into an inferno. They shared passionate, deep kisses as they stroked and tasted each other.

With a groan, Jasper finally pulled away. If he didn't stop now, there would be no turning back and he'd be making sweet love to her all night long until she called out his name.

Courtney's eyes sprang open. "What's wrong?"

"Nothing, baby," Jasper whispered softly. "I thought you wanted to see the island, but if you'd rather I take you to bed, I'd be more than willing."

A rose blush spread across Courtney's fair skin, and her polished jade eyes shone at him. "You're right. I don't know what came over me."

"Don't apologize," Jasper said. "I rather enjoyed your aggressiveness. But Punta Cana does have some nice treasures I think you might like to enjoy during your visit."

Jasper had a point. "I would like to see some sights, other than my bedroom and this resort."

"I thought we'd start off first at a local dive bar by the beach here in town called Captain Cook's. It may not look like much on the outside so don't expect any fancy sauces or elaborate presentations like at the resort, but I promise you it has some of the freshest seafood around. We'll have some beers and maybe a Rum Runner before heading to the Bávaro Disco."

Courtney gave Jasper a wink. "Sounds like you've thought of everything."

"Not everything. Just save some energy for what I have in store for you later tonight." And with that comment, he took her by the hand and pulled her toward the door.

"Wait, wait," Courtney said, grabbing her clutch purse from the cocktail table. Seconds later they were out the door.

"Boy, you weren't lying," Courtney stated when they made it to Captain Cook's. The position right on the beach was great, but it looked as if she were walking into someone's garage. Large outdoor grills were near the entrance, and the plastic tables underneath palm-frond gazebos weren't much to speak of. There were large bathtubs filled with ice and all kinds of seafood, from lobster to shrimp to crab, all caught fresh from the sea.

"You can pick whatever you want," Jasper said, "and they'll cook it for you."

"Is this sanitary?" Courtney asked from his side, looking down in the tub.

"Trust me, okay?" Jasper gave her hand a squeeze. "I wouldn't poison you. This place has been around a long time. C'mon." He pulled her toward the entrance. "Let's have a beer."

"Isn't there any air-conditioned seating?" Courtney asked. She was sweltering after the ride in Jasper's truck, which didn't have a working a/c unit.

"Don't tell me you care about a little sweat?" Jasper asked. Because he could remember she was sweating plenty the other morning when he was buried deep inside her, and she was rising to meet his every thrust.

"I don't mind it in the right moment," Courtney clarified, "but I don't like to sweat over my food."

"There are fans outside," Jasper said, and led her to a palm-frond gazebo. They passed by a local band that was coming by each gazebo and serenading them. "You're going to live like a local."

From where they were on the beach, Courtney could see the yachts moored off the beach and sunbathers and tourists on their Jet Skis and WaveRunners.

Once they were seated, Jasper ordered a variety of grilled lobster, shrimp and calamari off the menu along with some ice-cold beer.

Although she appreciated a man who took the lead, Courtney couldn't resist commenting, "I am capable of ordering for myself."

"I realize that," Jasper replied, "but I know some of their best menu items. If you like I can get the waitress back."

"No need," Courtney said. "I trust your judgment."

"You just wanted me to know you could."

"Exactly." She pointed at him.

"Why are you so desperate to be taken seriously, Courtney? Don't you get enough of that in the real world?" As soon as he said the words, Jasper realized he'd let the cat out of the bag that he knew her identity.

"What do you mean? Do you know who I am?" Courtney searched his face for a sign of the truth.

Jasper struggled with whether he should lie or not, but considering he already wasn't playing fair about his true identity, he thought better of digging himself farther in the hole. "I happened to overhear the staff mention that you're a model is all." In truth, it was Miguel who'd told him, but he couldn't tell her that he'd been checking into her background.

Amusement flickered in Courtney's eyes. "I'm no model."

The waitress returned with their beer and set both bottles on the table.

"Cheers." Jasper held up his bottle and Courtney clicked hers against his. "So, why do you say you're not a model?"

"I'm a spokesmodel for my family's cosmetics company," Courtney replied.

Jasper bristled inside. "Oh and what does that entail?"

He wanted to appear curious and not give away that he knew more. His father's animosity toward the Adamses had nothing to do with him. Jasper held no ill will against her family, though he suspected Courtney might not see it that way.

"You mean beyond being a pretty face?" Courtney jeered. "My job is to increase product awareness. Usually I do this by making public appearances at special events, department stores, malls, clubs and trade shows, that sort of thing. The goal, of course, is to reach as many consumers as possible."

"So you're a party girl?" Jasper asked.

Courtney glared at him with reproachful eyes. His words had stung. "I resent what you're implicating, which is that I don't work hard." She was already very sensitive about this particular topic, because she felt her siblings didn't take her contribution to the company seriously. "Research has shown that a consumer's perception of a brand, product, service or company is profoundly affected by a live person-to-person experience. As a spokesmodel, I interact with many people at once to maximize a quantitative influence on consumer demand for our products." She sighed. "Why does everyone undervalue my contribution?"

"I'm sorry. I didn't mean to offend you." Obviously,

he'd hit a nerve. "I only meant that I imagine it can get pretty tiring."

"All that partying," Courtney added bitterly, taking a generous swig of her beer.

Jasper ignored her sarcasm. "No. I meant being in the public eye and constantly surrounded by people. I prefer my solitude."

"I'm used to it," she replied wearily. She'd become immune to her situation. How could she not after a decade of being AC's spokesmodel? But still, she was tired of being underappreciated. When she got back to the States, there were going to be some big changes at the company.

"If you ask me, sounds like you're ready to move on."

Had she given something away with her response? Courtney was good at hiding her emotions, even when she was tired or sick, because the show always had to go on. But now that Jasper had put a spotlight on her, she felt as if the cracks in her armor were showing.

After a long silence, Courtney finally said, "I do what's necessary for my family, but it might be time for me to step down."

"I'm sure you'll be great in your next role," Jasper said. With all the energy and vitality Courtney possessed, he was sure she would be successful in whatever she put her mind to.

"Thank you." She was surprised at Jasper's unexpected encouragement. "My sister and I talked before my trip here and I told her I wanted a larger role at the company that would utilize my marketing degree."

Jasper's left eyebrow rose a fraction. Clearly he was surprised she wasn't some spoiled airhead. She had a brain and had exercised it to obtain a degree. "And you, what are your aspirations, Jasper? You must know you can't rely solely on brawn and those strong muscles—" she reached across the table to stroke his biceps "—forever. What's your game plan?"

"To own my own construction company," Jasper returned, which was the truth. Only he'd accomplished that task nearly nine years ago and now had a rapidly expanding hotel empire.

The waitress returned with their combination platter of grilled shrimp and calamari, Captain Cook's fish brochettes, freshwater crab and lobster accompanied with a salad and French fries. They both dug into the shellfish, dipping the crab into the lime-flavored butter.

"Mmm…this is delicious." Courtney couldn't help moaning aloud.

"Told ya."

"There's nothing like owning your own business, my father always says," Courtney said, picking up where she'd left off. "He started off small, with just a vision, until it steadily grew into something more. Now it's something that he could pass on to his children, a legacy."

"I hear the admiration in your voice about your father," Jasper said. He was envious. He'd never felt that way about Andrew. Ever.

"Yeah, he's an amazingly gifted man whom I respect a lot," Courtney said. She was surprised she was having such a deep and profound conversation with Jasper, whom she'd just met. He was so easy to talk to and she could just be herself. It was a refreshing change of pace.

They finished off a good majority of the seafood platters and another round of beer before Jasper took her to the Bávaro Beach Resort. The resort was alive with tourists and gamblers. Jasper took Courtney to the Bávaro Disco inside the resort. With its flashing lights and high-octane music, it was one of the favorite clubs on the island. He was sure Courtney would like the place. He used his VIP status to get them into the upstairs lounge so they could enjoy the music but be away from the crowd. Upstairs, there were sleek leather sofas and lounge chairs and a bottle service for the VIPs.

"Do you know everyone in town?" As they made it up the flight of stairs, Courtney commented on how easily Jasper got them into the club. There was a long line of people waiting to get into the disco, but Jasper had walked up to the bouncer as if he owned the place, whispered something in his ear and the big, burly guard had pulled the rope so they could jump the line.

"What do you mean?" Jasper said, even though he knew exactly what she meant.

"You know what I'm talking about," Courtney said once they were upstairs and seated on lounge chairs. "First, you get a free room at the resort and now that bouncer downstairs just let you in? Does everyone in town owe you? Or you just have major connections?"

Jasper paused, thinking carefully about what he wanted to say. "I know how to treat people, and in return they do things for me."

"Is that so?" Courtney said. She was sure there was more to the story, but Jasper wasn't sharing with her. She noticed he hadn't shared much about himself. The only thing she knew was that he worked at a construction company, he was a fantastic lover and he was great with his hands and mouth. A shiver of desire ran up her spine at the memory of that mouth of his tracing her spine with his tongue.

"Yes," Jasper said. "We're benefiting from it, are we not?"

Courtney smiled. "I'm not complaining. Just curious about you, Jasper. You're an enigma."

"And that's a bad thing?"

"No, but I think you rather like it. It keeps people off-kilter not knowing exactly who you are."

Jasper's forehead creased. Courtney was very percep-tive. He did keep to himself and remained a mystery to most of his staff. He supposed it was because he wanted to be as far removed from Andrew Jackson as possible so the stench didn't rub off. Would he ever be far enough away?

"How about a drink?" he asked, changing the subject.

Courtney noticed that Jasper was comfortable talking about her, but when the subject turned to him he was quick to move on to a different subject.

"What would you like?" he asked when a busty waitress in short pants and a tank top came over to take their order.

"Oh, so you're asking me this time?"

"As I recall, the last time I tried to order for you, you weren't too pleased with me."

"I'll have a Miami Vice."

"Make that two," Jasper told the waitress.

"I like the music," Courtney said, getting up and sway-ing her hips to the beat of the music as she looked down at the crowd below. It was a mix of house and techno.

Jasper came up behind her and circled his arms around her waist and together their bodies swayed as one to the drumbeats. His large hands grasped hers and intertwined their fingers. Courtney leaned back and rested her head against his muscled shoulders and soaked in the moment.

When the waitress came, Jasper motioned to the table. "Just put them down, we'll get 'em."

When the music turned sultry, Courtney turned around and Jasper enveloped her in his arms, resting his hands above her hips, and they continued their dirty dancing as if they were the only couple upstairs, which they weren't. But to Courtney they were. When the song ended, they finally pulled away and Courtney used the break to sip on her drink and hopefully cool herself down. It did the reverse. The liquor spread through her veins like fire and warmed her from the inside out.

Jasper sat back in the lounger across from her and regarded her silently.

Courtney was keenly aware of his scrutiny. "Do I have something stuck in my teeth?" She reached for her purse.

"No, I was just admiring how beautiful you are," Jasper answered honestly. Her bone structure, high cheekbones and clear skin were flawless. Courtney was a stunningly beautiful woman with striking eyes that spoke to him. "So, who did you get that eye color from?"

"My mother. My brother and I favor her with our fair skin and green eyes, while my older sister is the spitting image of our father."

"Interesting dynamic," Jasper murmured, sipping his drink.

"And you? Who do you look more like?" Courtney asked, eager for some snippet of real information about Jasper.

Jasper wrinkled his nose. "My father."

Courtney noticed how he admitted that fact reluctantly. Clearly, there was no love lost between the two men. She would love to know more, but tonight was not about family. It was about them.

Several dances and two Miami Vices later, Courtney and Jasper abandoned the disco in favor of going back to the resort. Neither had said much on the ride home. They didn't need to because when they got to her room at the resort, their bodies spoke to each other.

Their passion for each other was uncontrollable, and they began stripping each other's clothes almost as soon as they walked into her room. They left a trail of clothes from her living room until they reached the master bedroom.

They met each other on top of the bed. Jasper quickly relieved himself of his briefs, while Courtney didn't have much on underneath her jumpsuit except a pair of bikini panties, which quickly got tossed over her shoulder.

Jasper swept her, weightless, into his arms and crushed her to him. His mouth sought hers hungrily and she met his fiery kiss with demands of her own. She pressed her lips eagerly against his with a tantalizing series of slow, searing kisses. His lips parted and she kissed him long and hard, savoring every delicious moment.

Courtney wrapped one leg and then another across Jasper's waist until they were in a seated position. Jasper slid his hand down her silky, soft back while the other hand gently outlined the circle of her breast. He seemed enthralled by her soft curves and bent down to take one erect nipple between his lips. He circled the bud with his tongue, nipped it with his teeth and sucked on it until Courtney shivered in his arms.

Jasper loved each nipple as if they were sweet, dark morsels in a chocolate-chip cookie. "Every time I look at you, your nipples will harden," Jasper warned as he tongued the other nipple.

Courtney had no doubt her body would remember every response Jasper evoked in her of its own volition.

His mouth returned to hers and his thrusting tongue roused her passion, but she wasn't the only one being swept away; she could feel Jasper growing hard.

He continued to touch her until he found her damp, hot secret place between them both. He teased the slick folds with his fingers and Courtney couldn't resist uttering a shocked cry as intense pleasure radiated through her. When he flicked the nub at the center of her, she nearly jumped off the bed, but that didn't stop him from lazily dallying with her core in a delicious rhythm. She felt like a musical instrument that only Jasper could play. He knew exactly what chord to strike for a sigh or moan to escape her tremulous lips. It didn't take long for her orgasm to come, swift and strong, and she threw her head back exultantly and fell against the bed.

Jasper was thrilled that he could elicit that kind of reaction from Courtney. He rose from the bed and looked down, drinking in the sight of her. In the moonlight coming through the terrace doors, he could plainly see her features and her shapely curves. He wasn't sure one week with her would be enough to enjoy her the way he wanted.

"You are so beautiful," he said huskily.

"You make me feel beautiful." Courtney drew in a ragged breath at the longing in his gaze.

Jasper quickly reached for a condom that he'd taken the liberty of removing from his pants pocket and sheathed himself before cupping Courtney's butt and pulling her toward him. He slid easily inside her warm, waiting body, desperate to claim her as his.

The feeling of him inside her must have made Courtney want more because she wiggled her hips against his shaft.

"Like that?" he murmured.

"Oh, yes."

He rewarded her by placing his hands possessively around her hips and moved her, guiding himself in and out. Their bodies instinctively increased the pace and soon their mutual desire gathered a storm and threatened to overtake them.

But Jasper didn't let it. He changed positions by pulling Courtney atop him so she could ride him like a stallion. He wanted to watch her scandalous responses. He loved when she squatted on her ankles above him and took him in, squeezing her core tightly around him as her pert breasts bobbed up and down.

Their fused energies lit up the bedroom, and the intensity spread through her like wildfire. Courtney's orgasm came first and she exploded above him. "Oh my…" she murmured.

Jasper was close behind her, gripping her hips roughly, and two hard thrusts later, he went rigid beneath her.

The strange sensation she felt when she raised her head to look down at him scared the heck out of her. She'd never felt this way after making love before. It had felt so good and so right she'd almost cried. *Good Lord,* she had to get a hold of herself. It was just sex. She was here for fun and sun. Nothing more.

Jasper was quite satisfied having Courtney sitting on his lap. He'd enjoyed their lovemaking because she was uninhibited and responsive. He tenderly touched her cheek with his fingers and gave her a gentle kiss.

Chapter 5

It was 5:00 a.m. and Courtney was completely exhausted. She hadn't gotten much sleep the night before with Jasper staying over, but she had a photo shoot to get to.

When she arrived, the photographer was already setting up several stands, an umbrella, reflector and soft-lighting boxes for several of the photos that would be featured in Bliss's new campaign. It was a little chilly first thing in the morning, but his assistant thankfully handed her a cup of coffee, which Courtney drank liberally.

She wasn't pleased to have to sit in the hair and makeup chair as extensions were added to her short hair, but doing this was a necessary evil. Her family hadn't been too happy when she'd chopped off her hair a couple of years ago, but she'd been tired of the long hair and wanted a new, edgier look. Of course, it was moments like this, when she had to sit for well over an hour while the hairdresser added extensions, that were no fun, but at least when it was over she didn't have to live with it for long. Once the shoot was over, they would come out, but she had to admit the long honey-blond extensions looked good. They hung in wavy curls down her back, and they would be perfect for blowing in the wind, the photographer had said.

The makeup artist completed the look by adding soft, natural foundation to her face, a light gloss to her lips and sparkly eye shadow and mascara to her eyes.

Courtney wasn't looking forward to the bikini portion. She hated her curves and always wanted to lose another five pounds. Not to mention that she'd eaten like a cow with Jasper the night before at Captain Cook's. Reluctantly, she slid into her bikini and when she was done, she came and stood in front of the photographer.

"Do I pass muster?" she asked, spinning around on her heel.

"You'll do." He smiled. Though his appreciative glance said otherwise.

"Where is the male model?" Courtney inquired when he began taking photos of her.

"Came down with a case of food poisoning," the photographer said. "We'll have to do those shots tomorrow."

Courtney wasn't happy about that, since she'd been hoping to have tomorrow to herself.

"We're going to do all your bikini shots first while the sunrise is coming up. Then I'll have you change into resort wear at the end."

"Gotcha!" Courtney gave him a salute. "Where would you like me?"

For the next hour Courtney worked her magic. She didn't see Jasper come down to the beach to watch her.

He'd woken up in her bed half an hour ago and found her gone but then remembered she'd mentioned an early-morning photo shoot. A pang of guilt had surged in him for keeping her up so late and not allowing her to get her beauty rest. But then again the sex they'd shared last night had been nothing short of explosive and one time hadn't been enough. After a short nap, he'd awoken her and they'd made love again until he heard her soft cries of pleasure.

Blinking, Jasper focused on Courtney ahead. From his vantage point, he could see her in a skimpy bikini. It was a zebra print with gold-plated detail at the shoulder and hip. He watched as she easily glided through several poses: splashing in the water, kneeling in the sand, lying in the sand while running her fingers through her hair.

Her hair was much longer. They must have added some extensions, he thought, but that only added to her allure. When she rose to sit in the sand with her chin in her hand and put her fingers in her mouth, his groin tightened in response.

What was wrong with him? He was acting like some infatuated teenage boy watching his crush from afar. The thing was, he couldn't look away and he doubted any man, heck, any woman, who saw her would be able to without wanting to know what she was selling.

He would love to stay and watch her work, but he had to get to work himself. He had to see exactly what was going on at his hotel site. Otherwise, Palace at Punta Cana would never get off the ground.

Later that afternoon, after he'd worked at the construction site, Jasper showered at his villa and made his way back to the resort. He'd noticed that the crew seemed to stop working at 3:00 p.m., which left him more time for Courtney, but definitely meant they were slacking. He'd reviewed the foundation materials used and felt they were inadequate, but the loan inspector had signed off for Dorchester to continue. Jasper was going to have to bide his time until he found something more incriminating. He was walking through the resort when Miguel stopped him.

"Sir, is everything okay?" he asked. Jasper was known for stopping by the resort unexpectedly, but he'd been dropping by a lot more the past few days.

"Of course, Miguel," Jasper replied, patting the man's shoulder. "You remember that matter I mentioned the other day?"

"Yes, sir."

"Well, I need you to keep up the charade, ol' boy. To everyone here, I'm just a hardworking construction worker."

"Of course."

Jasper spied Courtney walking through the lobby. When she saw him, she began walking over. Jasper had to admit no one could wear a pair of shorts quite like Courtney. She was wearing a bikini top and a skimpy pair of cream shorts that stopped dangerously close to the apex at her thighs, causing him to lust for those long, shapely legs of hers that went on for miles.

Jasper watched Miguel swallow beside him.

"What are you doing here?" Courtney asked. "I thought I wouldn't see you until later." She glanced down at her watch and saw that it read 4:00 p.m.

"I know," Jasper said. "We got off earlier than I thought."

"I was just about to go swimming." Courtney motioned down to her attire. After her photo shoot this morning, she'd had to come in and take a nap, but now she had her second wind. "Care to join me?"

Jasper looked down at his shorts and Bermuda shirt. He hadn't brought any swim shorts with him.

"I'm sure I could procure some swim shorts for you, sir, if you need them?" Miguel said from his side.

"Miguel, ol' boy." Jasper patted his manager's shoulder as if he were an old friend. "You wouldn't mind?"

Miguel smiled, catching on to the hint and playing along. "Of course not. I really appreciated the help you gave me with me adding that room in my house, so you know I've got your back."

"Thanks." Jasper shook his hand and Miguel walked away, leaving the two of them alone.

Courtney stepped back and folded her hands across her chest. "I don't know what it is, but everyone around this town seems to cater to your every whim."

"That's not true."

She raised an eyebrow. "I'm not imagining it, Jasper. Everyone seems powerless to say no to you."

Jasper drew her closer and whispered so that only she could hear him. "Would that include you?"

"Well, that would depend on what you want."

He grinned devilishly and Courtney just knew he was thinking something lascivious. She was about to respond, but Miguel returned with a bag and handed it to Jasper.

"I believe those should work for you," Miguel said. "If not, let me know." He inclined his head to the front desk clerk. "And she'll be happy to assist you."

"Thanks again, Miguel." Jasper shook his hand. "Ready for that swim?"

Courtney and Jasper did more than swim in the Olympic-size pool, which was one of three the resort had. They also went out to the beach and rode on WaveRunners. Courtney had always wanted to try one, but had been afraid to go out on her own, but with Jasper driving she knew she would be safe.

After putting on a life vest and wading in the ocean, Jasper hopped onto the Yamaha WaveRunner, and after lending her a hand to scoot behind him, he started the engine.

They were off in a flash, flying through the ocean waters, and Courtney enjoyed every minute of it, from the splash of the water to the wind in her face.

"I loved it!" Courtney said when the ride was over and they were back on dry land.

Jasper glanced at her cheeks that were flushed with excitement. With her coloring, he could read her pretty easily. "Glad you liked it," he said, helping her to remove her life vest.

"What's in store for tomorrow?" she asked. She was enjoying her adventures in Punta Cana.

"Hmm…" Jasper rubbed his goatee thoughtfully. "I'll think of something. In the meantime, I'm starved. How about a hot shower and some food?"

At the mention of food, her stomach grumbled. "I wholeheartedly agree."

An hour later, after a shower in her suite, they were having dinner in one of the five restaurants that the resort had. This time Courtney insisted she pay for the meal.

"You've already done so much," she said when he balked. "This is my treat." She was sure he didn't make much on his salary, and he'd already paid during most of their outings.

"Fine, this time." He'd reluctantly agreed to allow Courtney to pay, because he knew he couldn't keep spending so much money without her getting suspicious. It was just that Courtney wasn't the average woman he'd encountered, and he wanted to shower her with the best, but he'd put himself in an untenable position by lying to her about his profession.

At the time, it seemed innocent enough because he hadn't expected it to be anything other than a one-night stand. The joke had been on him, because one night with Courtney had turned into more, and he'd found he enjoyed the lady's company. And the feeling was mutual. He'd seen the way she'd lit up when she'd spotted him in the lobby earlier and he'd gotten an inner satisfaction from it.

Of course now he didn't know how to get himself out of the lie. He doubted Courtney would be happy to learn that he'd duped her because he'd thought her a superficial socialite.

"You ready to order?" Courtney said, breaking into his thoughts. The waiter was standing at the table ready to take their order.

"Uh, yes," Jasper answered. One of these days he would have to figure out a way to tell Courtney that he'd been less than truthful with her.

But between working at the construction site, stopping into the office and spending his evenings with Courtney, the moment had never presented itself.

After Courtney finished the second day of the photo shoot, he'd set about showing her the best of Punta Cana. Whether they were exploring another beach or throwing the dice at a hotel casino, she was impressed by his knowledge of the local culture.

One day, he took Courtney shopping at the Plaza Bávaro so she could browse the gift shops. Jasper found Courtney was great at bargaining with the locals. Watching her converse with them at ease, he forgot she'd been born with a silver spoon in her mouth.

Courtney was having fun milling around the shops and bargain shopping. She found several handmade souvenirs and ceramics for Kayla and her mother and hand-rolled cigars and rum for her father, Shane and Ethan.

She was so enraptured by her shopping that she didn't see Jasper leave the shop she was in. When she'd made her purchase and handed the shop owner several pesos, she walked outside to find Jasper.

She found him across the street surrounded by several children, who by their tattered clothes seemed homeless. Her eyes darted back and forth nervously, especially when she heard one of them ask, "Spare change? We real hungry."

"What's your name?" Jasper asked the youngster who couldn't be more than eleven or twelve years old. His face was smeared with dirt and his dark, straight hair looked as if it hadn't been combed in days.

"Diego."

Courtney was concerned when Jasper reached for his wallet in front of the children. What if they snatched it and ran away? It wasn't as though Jasper was rich and could afford the loss. If he tried to chase them, he was outnumbered. But Jasper didn't seem to have any fear and continued to interact with them.

Cautiously, Courtney waited a safe distance on the other side of the street, but close enough that she could hear Jasper ask them several questions about their parents.

"Died during a hurricane," Diego said.

"How are you surviving?" Jasper inquired.

"Kindness of strangers," the boy replied. "My friends and I were in the same village that got wiped out. We hate the orphanage, so we left."

His story tore at Jasper's heartstrings and he put his wallet away. "Come with me." He started to lead them to his favorite hole-in-the-wall restaurant down the road when he noticed Courtney standing across the street. "C'mon," he said. "They won't bite."

Reluctantly, Courtney started toward them. "This is Señora Courtney," Jasper told Diego, who appeared to be the leader.

"Señora." The boy inclined his head.

"We're going to get you boys something to eat." Jasper smiled at Courtney as he led the way to the restaurant.

"Are you sure about this?" Courtney whispered in his ear.

"Yeah. Don't worry. These kids just need a helping hand."

A short walk later, they arrived at a Mexican restaurant, and while the children settled themselves at several tables, Courtney watched Jasper speak with the owner of the dive. She watched him open his wallet and tuck several bills into the pocket of the owner's shirt. Soon a waitress was coming to the table and taking the children's order.

Jasper returned with a satisfied smile on his face.

"Don't tell me you have an arrangement with this owner too?" Courtney raised a brow. She was having a hard time buying that Jasper knew this many people.

"No, I don't." Jasper shook his head. "But I gave him enough money to feed the children for a week or so until I can give him some more money."

"What will you do?"

Jasper shrugged. "I'll make do."

Courtney was touched by Jasper's generosity. He didn't know these children, but he was willing to go without in order for them to be fed. If she had any preconceived notions about Jasper being unrefined, she'd been completely wrong. He was a strong, honorable man who when he saw someone in distress couldn't resist helping out. Look how they had met. She had been stranded on the side of the road and he'd helped her. Despite herself, Courtney's heart began pounding in an erratic rhythm and her pulse quickened. This wasn't good. She was starting to feel something for Jasper. She was just supposed to be having an island fling, and if that had turned into something more, what exactly would that mean?

* * *

"What's going on down there, Courtney?" Kayla asked from the other end of the line later that afternoon.

Heck, Courtney wished she had the answer to that question. Her fling with Jasper was becoming more than she had bargained for. But instead she said, "What do you mean?"

"Don't play coy," Kayla replied. "It doesn't become you. I heard your shoot for Bliss is over, but you're still in the Dominican Republic. Why?"

"Sorry," Courtney said. It was true that she'd finished the photo shoot a few days ago, but she had gotten so caught up with Jasper that she had forgotten to contact her family. "I decided spur of the moment to take a vacation."

"That's fine." Kayla sighed on the other end. "But I just wish you had let me or Shane know. We were worried about you. Mother called me and told me you hadn't returned home when expected, and I wanted to make sure you were all right."

Courtney felt bad. She would never want her family to worry about her. "I'm truly sorry. I'll be sure to contact you guys next time. Scout's honor."

"It's okay," Kayla said. "It was just so unlike you. We wondered what had gotten into you." The question should have been, who had gotten into her? His name was Jasper and he had her mind spinning. They had spent the past few days together and she wasn't nearly tired of him yet as she typically was with other men. It was as if he'd cast a spell over her.

"I guess too much fun and sun," Courtney said after a long pause.

Kayla laughed, hoping to ease some of the tension out of their conversation. "So, how is Punta Cana? I heard it's beautiful this time of year."

"It's great."

"So, how much longer do you think you'll be staying?"

"Oh, I don't know. Another few days," Courtney replied offhandedly. "It's been nice not having any public appearances and having to get all dressed up. I can just be myself."

"I thought you liked being in the public eye," Kayla said. That's what she'd always thought. Of course, before her trip Courtney had indicated she wanted more.

"I did," Courtney replied. "I mean, I do, but as I told you before, I need to make some changes and I'll be ready to discuss them with you when I get back."

"Okay." Kayla would never deny her sister a larger role at the company. Adams Cosmetics was a family business.

"Well, I have to run." Courtney wanted to get off the phone before Kayla could ask any more questions. Other than Tea, she didn't want to tell anyone else about Jasper, at least not yet. She just wanted to savor the experience without any questions or comments from the peanut gallery. "See you soon." She hung up the phone.

On Sunday, Jasper's day off from Dorchester's, he decided to take Courtney on a horseback ride up to spectacular El Limón Waterfall in the Samana Peninsula. If he was by himself, he would have hiked it, but with the rough terrain and heat, Jasper knew Courtney would be better off on horseback.

"Are you enjoying the scenery?" Jasper asked from his horse as he turned behind him to check on Courtney.

"It's beautiful!" Courtney enjoyed the fern-lined trail along the Limón River with its low-hanging trees and thatched huts along the route. It was a beautiful path in a tropical rainforest.

They arrived at the waterfall after a short hike down the path, and the view took Courtney's breath away. The waterfall was nestled deep in a thick palm forest and, according to their guide, rose nine hundred feet above sea level and cascaded 150 feet into a deep pool of water below.

"You wanna swim?" Jasper asked.

"In front of all these people?" Courtney asked. Several tourists were milling about taking pictures, but only a few had ventured out into the water.

"Don't tell me you're afraid of people watching you? Isn't your bathing suit underneath those shorts?"

"Yes."

"Then let's do it!" Jasper flung the T-shirt he'd been wearing over his head and pulled down his shorts to his swim shorts. "See you inside." And with that comment, he dived into the water.

Courtney debated with herself whether to join him. The water did look inviting and it was hotter than Hades outside. What would it hurt? She shimmied out of her shorts and tank and dived in after Jasper.

They swam away from the crowd into a small alcove underneath the waterfall to make out. With the water cascading in front of them, Jasper lowered his head and with his mouth invited Courtney to come play. He brushed his mouth across hers, slowly and deliberately. Momentum built as neither broke the kiss. They couldn't.

Their tongues mated and danced as they feasted on each other with gentle nips and licks. Jasper's hands were hot as he skimmed his hand down her spine and cupped her buttocks, pressing her closer to him. Courtney took the hint and wrapped her legs around his waist.

Jasper kissed her mouth and then her neck before moving to her breasts. He squeezed the mounds, and a moan escaped her lips. Her head fell back when she felt his mouth on her nipple through her swimsuit. It hardened as if on cue, and her back arched when he took the bud in his mouth and rolled it around with his tongue.

"That's enough for now. We'll have to finish this later on," Jasper whispered huskily, and set her back onto the river floor. He could feel the heat emanating from her core, but more importantly he was getting hard and might take her right underneath the falls with the tourists only a stone's throw away.

Courtney was hazy with desire and couldn't see clearly. Just a touch from Jasper had her acting like a wanton woman in the middle of a very public waterfall. "Yes, let's," she said, forcing herself to move and make her way back to the shore.

Chapter 6

They dressed quickly and after the hike up to the horses, they were back on the trail. When they made it back to Jasper's old, beat-up truck, which Courtney had gotten rather used to, neither one of them said a word. They didn't have to. They had become good at reading each other's minds, and Courtney knew as he did that there wouldn't be any visiting local watering holes tonight for dinner. They would be each other's dinner.

Courtney wondered how long it would take for the passion she felt for Jasper to die out. Would it take a few more days? They'd been together over a week now and it didn't seem to be dying down. Instead, it had gotten stronger with time. What was wrong with her? She wasn't the type to get emotionally attached. What was it about this man that she found hard to resist? Was it his raw sex appeal?

Courtney didn't ponder it for too long because when they made it back to the resort and to her suite, there was no more time for thought. There was only time for action. When he stepped toward her, her pulse kicked into high gear and her heart soared. Their bodies collided with aching and a need that had yet to be fulfilled.

"You feel so good," he said as his hands dived into her hair.

Courtney's hands gripped at his T-shirt and she lifted the offending garment from his pliable body and flung it across the room. "I want you. I want to feel you inside me. I want you to take me to the edge...."

Jasper drew in an unsteady breath seconds before he claimed her lips, crushing her to him. His lips were hard and firm over hers, demanding a response, and Courtney gave him her assent by giving herself freely to his kiss.

She reached for the waistband of his shorts and helped relieve him of his shorts and swim shorts. Courtney gloried in his male splendor. He was so magnificent and strong that she couldn't resist grazing her soft fingers across his stomach and near his growing erection. Jasper shuddered underneath her.

"Tease."

Courtney looked up at him. "Oh, don't you worry, there's more where that came from."

"Good, because I have something in store for you too." Jasper yanked down her shorts and bathing suit bottom in one fell swoop. Then he reached behind her to loosen the strings that held up her bikini top and discarded the scrap of material until she was as naked as he was.

"So what do you have in store for me this time?" she inquired.

"I'm sweeping you off your feet," Jasper answered, lifting her into his arms and walking toward the bed. He set her down on the bed and then knelt between her legs. He glanced up and gave her a wicked smile as he parted her thighs and lowered his head.

When he flicked his tongue across her womanly lips, Courtney lifted her hips to give him better access.

"Hold on, woman," he said. "It's going to be a long ride."

He commenced with conquering her with his wicked tongue that he used to lick, flick and tease. Courtney could hear her whimpers over his lovemaking but was powerless to silence them. Jasper didn't stop his pleasuring at her cries. Instead he held her hips firmly in place and continued his erotic feasting. She came undone when he thrust two long fingers inside her. That's when she bucked, screamed out his name and fell spent against the pillow.

Courtney had never felt such intense pleasure in her entire life. She glanced up and found that Jasper had a satisfied grin on his face.

"You don't play fair," she murmured.

"Now, that wouldn't be any fun, would it?"

"Just you wait." Courtney pointed a finger at him. "Your turn is next."

Jasper smiled like the Cheshire cat. "I can't wait."

She rose on her shins and pushed him back against the pillows. She licked her lips first, and then she bent forward and pressed her mouth to the head of his penis. Jasper wanted to explode right from that tiny action, but he didn't. Instead, he waited as her mouth enveloped him. She sucked him forcefully and with intent, bobbing her head up and down, desperate to make him come as she had.

He gripped at the sheets when she suddenly pulled away. "Don't stop…."

He was a goner when she took him back into her mouth again, but this time even farther. "Courtney…!" She licked and sucked him, all the while stroking him, until Jasper was close to losing all self-control. That's when she pulled away.

Courtney sat back on her haunches. "There, I think I have repaid you in equal measure."

"You little minx!"

"And you love it," Courtney said. "But don't think you're finished, because I have more in store for you."

Despite the teasing grin on Courtney's mouth, somehow Jasper remembered to grab for protection. He was glad he did because she lowered her body onto his waiting erection and took him deep inside her.

She was hot and slick for him, so the glide inside her was easy. An agonizing groan escaped his lips. She moved her hips, wrapped her legs on either side of him and slowly rocked against him.

"Any slower and I'm going to die," he murmured.

What came next scared Jasper. She drew him in and out of her body so intensely that he felt her drawing into his body, his soul, his mind. He hadn't expected such a strong connection to Courtney, but how could he not? When he wasn't working, they'd spent every day and night together. That had to be what it was.

Courtney increased the tempo of her rocking until she bucked and undulated against him.

Jasper sat up and kissed her then. She allowed him to play with her mouth and gather her against him. He relished the contact of Courtney's pert breasts clutched against him. He bent his head down so he could boldly suck on one brown nipple while his fingers went to her womanly lips and he inserted his fingers between them. He lazily moved them until gasps of pleasure escaped her lips and she arched her back as her orgasm shook through her entire being. That's when Jasper swayed forward, thrusting harder…twisting…riding the wave as he too crested to completion. When he did, he gave a loud, exultant shout of joy.

But Jasper didn't allow her to rest for long because they were too tempted by each other. He turned her over so that she was kneeling in front of the headboard and he took her from behind.

Courtney found the position intoxicating, especially when Jasper licked her spine or teased her breasts or played with the flesh at the apex of her thighs. He quickened the rhythm and soon she was swooning as the force of his swift thrusts sent both of them careening toward another orgasm.

She'd loved the way…no, wait, where had that word come from? She *liked* when Jasper enveloped her in the cocoon of his arms and entwined his fingers with hers. After they'd made love, Courtney relished his nearness. How was she going to be able to leave this man when it came time for her to go back to Atlanta, back to her life? She was addicted.

Jasper continued his quest to show Courtney the island. He took her zip-lining and initially Courtney resisted because she was scared of heights. She didn't want to go, but Jasper convinced her it would be great fun. After she'd gotten over her fear and climbed the ladder to the first zip line and then let go on the first zip, she'd enjoyed it.

Afterward, she wanted to do it again, but her stomach growled. They feasted on a local dish of *sancocho*. Courtney enjoyed the rich stew of chicken, pork, pumpkin, yucca, plantain, corn on the cob and cilantro. She ate it with a hearty portion of rice and sliced avocado, the traditional sides. Courtney found that she was letting down her guard and enjoying the culture. Although Jasper had thought she was a pampered princess, she was proving to him that she wasn't above enjoying life's simple pleasures. It was what he'd learned to do as a teenager growing up on the farm.

Later that night after they made love and were lying in each other's arms in bed, Jasper confided to Courtney about what he suspected was going on at the hotel's construction site. He said that he thought the owner, Jim Dorchester, was using subpar materials, such as bad concrete. He'd already seen an order of non-flame-retardant lumber that he was going to have to stop.

"What are you going to do about it?" Courtney inquired.

"I don't have enough proof yet," Jasper replied. "I need someone who is willing to come forward. Dorchester could claim the order was a mistake."

"Do you think you can convince someone to rat out Dorchester?" Courtney asked. "They could lose their job."

"I know it's a long shot, but think about the alternative. Someone could get hurt in the long run if this hotel is constructed poorly."

"That's very honorable."

"It's the right thing to do," Jasper said emphatically.

"I love it when you're passionate." Courtney's eyes blazed fire. "I wish more people were like you. We had a saboteur at my family's company last year."

"Really, what happened?" Jasper asked, even though he knew the answer to the question.

"My brother-in-law's ex-girlfriend snuck into my brother's lab and stole the formula to one of our fragrances."

"How did she get away with something like that?"

"She used her looks to beguile our security guard and when his back was turned, she took his access card to the lab. Then a safecracker came with her to crack my brother's safe."

"Wow! That's pretty underhanded. So, what happened to her?"

"Well, it took us a while to figure out, but once we did, we pressed charges, but the thing is...she was a famous actress and since this was her first offense, she got off with a slap on the wrist. We know she wasn't working by herself, but she refused to give up her accomplice."

"Who was it?"

"We're almost positive that it was our family's most bitter rival and competitor, Andrew Jackson of Jax Cosmetics."

Jasper wished he hadn't asked. Hearing his father's name caused Jasper's mouth to turn dry and a bitter taste to form. Not only was the bastard a bully, but he was also a thief. But Jasper wasn't surprised that Andrew Jackson had no morals. He'd heard rumors of his father's underhanded tactics from his mother as it had made all the local papers in Georgia.

But it also put him in an untenable position. He'd known that Courtney was a spokesmodel for her family's cosmetics company, but now he had confirmation of her real identity. Courtney wasn't some stranger. She was Courtney Adams.

The Adamses and Jacksons hated each other. If Courtney knew he was Andrew's son, she would jump out of his bed so fast his head would spin. He didn't want that. He was forced to continue the lie he'd perpetrated from day one. What else could he do?

"Never heard of him," he finally said.

"Of course, how would you?" Courtney shrugged. "You're not in the States. Plus I doubt the machinations of two cosmetics companies interests you much." She turned to face him. "But I've been curious—how did you come to live here?"

"Oh, that." Jasper was caught off guard. Of course she would want to know how he came to be on the island.

"Well, I came down here with some friends for a vacation about five years back and fell in love with place."

"You don't miss the States?" she asked. Jasper wasn't sure if she was asking out of curiosity or if there was more to the question. Was she wondering if he would leave Punta Cana to come visit her? Would she even want him to?

"Sometimes," Jasper answered honestly. "I visit on occasion to see my mother."

"Oh, of course." Courtney nodded in understanding.

"Are you getting anxious to get back to your life?" Jasper wondered. He sure hoped not, because he was enjoying having Courtney here. If he admitted it to himself, he'd shut himself off too much from the world and focused on building his hotel empire to the exclusion of his personal happiness. And now that Courtney was here, she'd shined a light on just how important human contact really was. "I realize life here in Punta Cana must be a slower pace than you're used to."

"It is, but I like it here," Courtney replied. "As crazy as it sounds, it kind of feels like a second home."

Jasper smiled broadly. He knew exactly what she meant because once he had come to DR, he'd known that he wanted a hotel in Punta Cana. Once Sea Breeze Resorts was complete, he'd decided to stay on for a while. Who knew that so many years later, he would still be there? "I'm glad you like it here."

"Well, that could be due to a certain attractive chocolate-skinned brother I met a couple of weeks ago," Courtney murmured, caressing her hands across Jasper's broad chest and stroking his nipples with her fingertips. He shuddered underneath her touch.

"Oh yeah?"

"Absolutely," Courtney said. "Kiss me."

And he did. A powerful, potent kiss that pierced through her being. Soon Courtney drifted off to sleep with a satisfied smile.

"We need you back home," Shane told Courtney a few days later. She'd just been preparing to go for a long run on the beach when her cell phone rang.

"Why? What's wrong?" Was it their parents? Had something happened?

"Andrew Jackson."

Courtney looked up to the ceiling. "Lord, what did he do now?"

"We've all been waiting for him to put out his imitation fragrance of Ecstasy at a lower price," Shane began. "And now he finally did. He waited until the bad press with Noelle Warner died down before introducing his knockoff."

"Enough said," Courtney said. "I'll be on the first flight out."

"Thank you, sis. I've already notified the pilot and he'll be there in an hour."

"Wow! You sure didn't give me much time."

"I'm sorry, but this came up rather suddenly and we're doing damage control. Ethan had been keeping tabs on Jax Cosmetics, but Andrew was sneaky and kept this hidden pretty well. We only just got word that they would be debuting the knockoff this week."

"No worries. I'll be back soon." Courtney sighed when she hung up the phone. That gave her just enough time to pack her bags and get to the airport. What it didn't leave her was time to go see Jasper and explain. She could call him, but she was terrified that saying goodbye would be just too hard. After all, they'd known this was an island fling and nothing more. Wasn't it better she pulled the bandage off quick versus the torturous aspect of drawing things out?

Courtney rushed to the closet to find her oversize suitcase and started unceremoniously throwing items of clothing and shoes in. She hated to leave. She was having so much fun in Punta Cana with Jasper that she'd forgotten she had a life in Atlanta waiting for her. She couldn't stay here forever living a fantasy and neglecting her family duties. Plus, she would never move up in the company if she didn't show her family she had real ideas that could make an impact on AC. This crisis with Jax Cosmetics was a prime example of what she could do to show her worth to her family.

Of course that didn't stop her from feeling like a total heel for leaving without so much as a word to Jasper. He'd been nothing but kind and respectful to her, more so than any other man ever had. Perhaps that was the problem, she told herself. Jasper had come to mean more to her than she had ever expected. She'd come to Punta Cana looking for an island fling with no attachments and what she'd found was an attractive, passionate, down-to-earth, funny and kind man. She couldn't forget what he'd done for those homeless kids at the Plaza.

Which was why leaving was so difficult. She didn't want to admit it, but deep down she knew she'd fallen fast for Jasper. She would miss him terribly, but she had to go.

She stopped packing long enough to make a quick call downstairs to Miguel to ask him to send a car within the hour. He was surprised she was leaving so quickly, but promised to have a car waiting for her.

An hour later, Miguel was tucking her into the Lincoln Town Car that was to take her to the airport. "A note for Mr....uh...Jasper?" Miguel asked.

Tears sprang to her eyes and Courtney shook her head.

"It's better this way, Miguel. You and I know this wouldn't last forever. Thank you for your hospitality. I enjoyed my stay."

As Miguel closed the door behind her, he drew in a deep breath.

"What do you mean she's gone?" Jasper said. When he'd gone to Courtney's hotel suite and found his staff cleaning it for the next guest, he'd been floored. What the hell had happened? Had she somehow found out he was Andrew's son? She couldn't have, he told himself as he stormed to the main building. He'd been so careful. He flung open Miguel's office door.

"Sir!" Miguel stood up, startled.

"Where is she?" Jasper roared.

"I'm sorry, Mr. Jackson." Miguel went back to calling him by his proper name. "But Ms. Adams checked out this morning."

"Why in God's name didn't you contact me?" Jasper asked.

"There wasn't time, sir," Miguel responded. "Ms. Adams checked out rather quickly and then there was an emergency here at the resort."

Jasper let out a ragged breath. How could this be? How could Courtney be gone? "Did she leave a note?" Jasper turned his dark, blazing eyes on the hotel manager.

"I'm sorry, sir, but no, she did not."

"She didn't leave a note?" Jasper said aloud, more for himself than Miguel. After everything they'd shared, she didn't even think him worthy of a note? He pulled out his cell phone to check for voice mail, but there was none. Courtney had left Punta Cana and him without so much as a backward glance.

For the first time in his life, Jasper was speechless. He

sank into the chair opposite Miguel's desk. He'd thought they'd come to mean more to each other in their short time together than just a roll in the hay, but he'd been wrong. Courtney had come for an island fling and nothing more. She'd shown that by her callous disregard of him. He didn't know what he was more upset by, that she'd tired of him and just didn't want him or that she'd left without a note.

Jasper rose from the chair. He would not take this lying down. Despite his less than forthrightness, he wouldn't let the pampered princess get away with treating him like the gum on the bottom of her shoe. Just because she thought he was a lowly construction worker did not give her the right to treat him so carelessly. He was determined to show her that he would not be trifled with. He would make her want him, and when she was pleading for more, he would walk away.

Chapter 7

"I'm so happy to have you back, darling." Elizabeth Adams kissed her daughter Courtney when she came strolling into the living room later that afternoon. Courtney noted that the entire family was in attendance, ready for another round with Andrew Jackson, no doubt.

Courtney leaned back to peruse her mother. Had she gotten more beautiful since she was away? Her fair skin was just as smooth as ever with nary a wrinkle, her green eyes shone brightly and had she lost a few pounds? She was wearing her usual attire of slacks, cardigan set and pearls.

"Thank you, Mama. I'm happy to be back," Courtney lied. She wasn't at all happy. She felt horrible for leaving the way she did and now felt terribly guilty. *How must Jasper feel?* He was probably furious to realize she'd left without so much as a call or note. At least the breakup was swift, and Courtney doubted she'd ever see him again.

But it was hard knowing she couldn't share her thoughts and dreams, much less her nights, in his arms ever again.

"My darling, are you okay?" her mother asked, stepping away to regard her.

Courtney blinked several times. "Oh, yes, I'm fine."

"Glad you're back, sis." Shane rose from the couch he was seated on with Gabrielle to give Courtney a big hug.

"It feels like you've been away for an eternity," Gabrielle added. "I've missed talking to you, girlfriend."

Courtney smiled as the warm cloak of family surrounded her, allowing some of the grief she felt over leaving Jasper to dissipate. "Me too. So, bring me up to speed on what's going on with Jax Cosmetics."

"The fragrance is called Noelle, and it's debuting this week with much less fanfare than Andrew would have liked," Kayla spoke up from across the room. She and Ethan had arrived at the mansion earlier in the afternoon.

"It smells dangerously similar to Ecstasy," Shane added.

"We all knew this was coming," Ethan said. "At our launch party a few months ago, Shane smelled the knock-off. Andrew just held back his launch until all the criminal business with Noelle was over. What he doesn't know is that Graham International has also filed a civil complaint against her for damages."

"With the no contest on the breaking-and-entering charges, the civil suit will wipe her out," Kayla said with a smile.

"Perhaps then she'll be willing to play ball," Ethan said.

"I doubt it. She didn't want to give Andrew up then. Why should she now?" Byron, their father, spoke up. He stood tall and proud at the far side of the room, holding a glass of cognac. His mahogany skin seemed even darker when he was angry. He was wearing black trousers and a pullover sweater. "If I know Andrew, he gave her some deal on the back end."

"We need to put on a full media blitz surrounding Ecstasy," Courtney said, interrupting the conversation. "We need to go head-to-head with Jax Cosmetics once and for all."

Kayla turned to look at her baby sister. What had gotten her fired up all of a sudden?

"In my final act as Adams Cosmetics spokesmodel, I will pull out all the stops."

"Your final act?" her mother said. "You no longer want to be the AC woman?"

Courtney looked at her mother. "It's time I step down and let someone else take the reins on the spokesmodel front. And I have some great ideas to lead our future marketing and publicity campaigns."

Kayla smiled proudly at Courtney. She was happy to see that her time away had done her some good. She'd come back sure of herself and focused.

"Allow me to show you what I propose." Courtney stood up and walked over to her iPad, which she had resting against the mantel. Her time in Punta Cana had served her well. While Jasper was working, she had typed up her ideas on her iPad in preparation for her transition.

An hour later, it seemed her family was duly impressed with her media campaign and business acumen. She was back in the saddle!

Courtney met up with Tea for drinks later at Tea's apartment in Buckhead. Courtney needed to tell her best friend everything that had happened down in Punta Cana.

Tea arrived at the door looking sophisticated as usual in

a black-and-white kimono-sleeve top and black jeans. Her shiny Latina hair was swept in a casual ponytail to the side.

"Well, look who's returned to the land of the living," Tea said when she opened the door. She leaned in to give Courtney a quick kiss on the cheek and a hug and accept the bottle of wine Courtney had brought. "Since I haven't heard from you in two weeks, I was beginning to think we needed to send out a search party for you." She grabbed hold of one of Courtney's arms and escorted her into the living room. "I thought perhaps some fine Dominican had kidnapped you."

"It was a fine brother," Courtney replied, plopping onto the couch alongside Tea.

"Do tell, do tell. But first let me uncork this delicious bottle of wine you brought." She went off in the direction of the kitchen and returned five minutes later carrying two wineglasses. She handed one to Courtney and kept one for herself.

Courtney accepted the glass and took a sip first. The Merlot was perfect. "Jasper was everything I could have dreamed of," she sighed as her head leaned back on Tea's red leather sofa. "Tall, dark and handsome was on the menu."

"And did he serve it up to you?" Tea inquired.

Courtney smiled from ear to ear. "Oh, he served it and baked it until I was done."

Tea laughed. "Wow! Now I know where I need to go when I need to let off some steam."

"I can't describe how incredible this man was, in and out of bed. He was fun and took me zip-lining and on WaveRunners and horseback riding to waterfalls. But he was also supersmart and spoke Spanish and bargained with the locals. He even paid for homeless kids to eat, and oh yeah…he was an incredibly giving lover."

"No wonder you couldn't leave him." Tea was enraptured by Courtney's story. "Sounds like he put quite a spell on you."

Courtney nodded. "I think I'm sprung, Tea. I can't stop thinking about him. His laugh, his smile, the way he looked at me when he…" She stopped herself from becoming too intimate.

"Given your feelings, I'm amazed you were able to face him," Tea said, drinking her wine. "How did he feel when you told him you were leaving?"

Courtney lowered her head and was silent for several minutes. She put down the wineglass on the cocktail table. "I didn't tell him."

"What do you mean you didn't tell him?"

"Well…Shane called and told me the private jet would be there in an hour and there just wasn't time."

"So you left the man without saying goodbye?"

"I know, I know, must you make me feel bad? I feel horrible enough already." Tears began to swim in Courtney's eyes as she replayed that moment in her head. In the end, she realized she'd taken the coward's way out. She knew if she'd had to face Jasper and tell him she was leaving, she wasn't sure she would have had the courage to leave.

"I'm sorry." Tea scooted closer to pat her knee. "I shouldn't have come down so harsh on you. Did you leave a note?"

Courtney shook her head violently before cradling it in her trembling hands. "You must think I'm cold and heartless. I just couldn't face him."

"Because you've fallen for him?"

Courtney looked up with red-rimmed eyes. "No, it can't be. I mean, I just like him a lot."

"Everything you've said tonight indicates otherwise," Tea said softly.

"Doesn't matter now, does it?" Courtney said. "We live in totally different worlds. I live here in Atlanta and he's a construction worker in Punta Cana. It would never work. This isn't *How Stella Got Her Groove Back*."

Tea shrugged. "If you say so. Of course, now you'll never know, since you didn't give the man the opportunity to stop you and say goodbye."

Courtney knew Tea was right. She would always wonder what could have been if she hadn't been afraid to put herself out there and tell Jasper that she was starting to fall for him.

"You want to fire the entire construction company?" Mark asked Jasper several days later. "Are you sure about that?" He'd noticed that Jasper was in a foul mood recently and had tried to steer clear, but when he'd been summoned into Jasper's office, he'd had to come.

"Yes, I want them out."

He'd seen enough. Since Courtney had left without a word, he'd been even more determined to wrap up his stint at Dorchester. So he'd remained on for a few more days, hoping for some proof. And he'd finally got it. Thanks to his rapport with the men on his crew, he'd finally found one laborer who'd overheard a conversation between the bank inspector and Dorchester and saw an envelope exchange hands. The man had agreed to come forward, provided Jasper could find some place for him should he lose his job. Jasper had agreed.

"You realize this will delay construction."

"I'm well aware of that," Jasper replied. "But with the information I've learned working there the last couple of weeks, I have grounds to terminate their contract."

"You know, Dorchester will fight you on this."

"Let him try," Jasper said. "I'll annihilate him." At the moment, he was itching for a fight. He was still smarting over Courtney leaving Punta Cana without so much as a call or a note. He hadn't quite wrapped his head around it, and his bad mood was exacerbated by the fact that he hadn't slept very well the night before. He told himself it was just a bout of insomnia, but his body knew why. He missed Courtney sleeping next to him. He missed the sleek curve of her body spooned next to him on the bed. It was funny how in a short span of time, she'd become an important fixture in his day.

Last night, when he'd gone back to his villa, he'd realized just how lonely he was without her. And it made him angry, angry that she hadn't given him the chance to say goodbye, to convince her to stay with him.

"Jasper, Jasper." Mark broke into his thoughts. "Did you hear what I just said?"

"Which was?"

"Do you have another construction company in mind you want me to reach out to?"

"Oh, yes." Jasper forced himself to return to the matter at hand. "Contact our second-lowest bidder and bring them in. See if you can convince them to come down on their price if they want the business."

"Will do." Mark rose to leave but stopped in his tracks. "And where will you be?"

"I will be in the States," Jasper responded. Just then

he'd decided that it was time he took care of some unfinished business. He was ready to give Courtney Adams a taste of her own medicine.

Chapter 8

"Your targeted approach to hit the Premiere Atlanta Beauty Show, the stylist show and the international trade shows for HBA and IBS with Ecstasy is a winning formula," Kayla told Courtney when they met up for lunch several days later. They'd decided to keep it simple and grab a salad at a local café. "Are you sure you're up to all this work before you step down?"

"Of course I am," Courtney replied. "I would never have suggested it if I wasn't up to the task." She needed the constant activity to keep her mind occupied and not thinking about Jasper. It was hard enough at the house each night with Shane and Gabby and watching them so deeply in love as they prepared for their wedding in less than two months. Courtney wondered if she'd ever have that. Or had she already had it? And she'd just let it slip through her fingers?

"Hmm...I wonder," Kayla said, taking a forkful of

salad. She was still trying to take off the last unwanted pounds of baby weight since her son Alexander's birth.

"Why do you say it like that?" Courtney asked.

"Because you don't seem yourself," Kayla replied. "Since you've got back you're focused on work, but you seem a little edgy. I would have thought all that fun in the sun would have mellowed you out."

"It did."

Kayla raised a brow. "Did something happen down there?"

"What do you mean?"

"I mean, did you meet someone?"

"I met a lot of people."

"Yes, but you decided to extend your trip, so who was he?" Kayla knew her sister well enough to know a man was involved. *How could it not be?* Her sister was a beautiful, sexy young woman. The men down there must have lost their heads.

"There was someone, but it ended and I'm back home." Courtney tried to downplay the affair, even though in her heart she knew that was far from the case. She'd left her heart back in Punta Cana and she hadn't felt the same since.

"Seems to me that it's not over," Kayla said thoughtfully. "At least not here." She pointed to Courtney's heart.

Courtney was surprised that her sister could still read her. Even though she'd married, had a child and moved away, the bond they'd created was still there. "You might be right," she finally admitted.

"Is there any chance things could work out?" Kayla asked.

Courtney shook her head. "No, his life is in Punta Cana and he seems very happy there." Jasper had created a comfortable, laid-back lifestyle away from the States. She doubted he wanted to come back to the rat race.

"I'm sorry to hear that." Kayla reached for her water glass and took a liberal sip. "I want you to be happy and if he made you happy, I'd want that for you."

Courtney reached across the table and squeezed her sister's hand. "Thanks, Kay. And in time, I will be." If she could forget a certain brother with a sexy goatee and ebony skin, she would be.

"Baby, I'm so happy to see you," Jasper's mother, Abigail Jackson, said, when he came to visit her on the Cartwright family farm several miles outside Marietta. "What are you doing here?" Her eyes brimmed with excitement. She was surprised he was there again so soon after his last visit.

"Can't a son come and check on his mama?" Jasper asked, bending down to give her a kiss. As he'd driven up, he'd stopped to check in with the caretaker he'd hired to keep an eye on the farm. Everything looked to be in order, and Jasper was pleased with his hire.

"Of course you can, sweetie," Abigail said, pushing several pillows back so she could sit up on her king-size bed. She was still convalescing from her spill on the steps when she'd broken her hip. She hated to be kept down. At fifty-two, she was still in good health because of the clean air, organic food and good living. "I've missed you. Come sit down." She patted a spot next to her on the bed.

Jasper did as instructed and grasped his mother's hand. "You're looking much better than the last time I saw you." At five foot three and a buck and a quarter, she was petite to begin with, so when she'd lost a few pounds, it had made her usual smooth skin appear slightly gaunt, but she was still as beautiful as ever to Jasper. She had a delicately carved oval face with kind brown eyes.

"Well, you know nothing is going to keep me down for long, son. So, tell me what's new with you. I know you didn't come back here just for me. Are you here on business?"

Jasper smiled. "It's personal."

"A lady friend? Perhaps?" Abigail inquired, staring into his midnight eyes. She sure hoped so. She'd been concerned that Jasper had become so focused on his career to the exclusion of everything else. She did want to be a grandma one day, but Jasper didn't seem interested in long-term relationships. If a woman had managed to turn his head, then she must be pretty incredible because Jasper wouldn't settle for mediocre.

"Yes, but she doesn't know who I am," Jasper answered honestly. He'd always been able to speak honestly with his mother, and he wasn't about to stop now. It probably came from the fact that they'd had so much to catch up on since he'd grown up without her. They'd been apart for almost a decade, thanks to Andrew, and Jasper didn't care to waste time.

"That you're Andrew Jackson's son?" Abigail knew instantly what he'd meant. From the moment he'd left her ex-husband's house, Jasper had been determined to distance himself as far as he could from Andrew. Why else would he have left the States to build hotels in the Caribbean?

Jasper nodded, rose from the bed and turned to face the window. "You know how I feel about that man." His eyes became dark and remote.

"He's still your father."

"That man doesn't know what it takes to be a father," Jasper replied, turning back around. "Or a human being for that matter. Look at his callous treatment of you. He used you as a human incubator so he could have an heir."

"And look where that got him," Abigail said. "A son who hates him and wants nothing to do with him or his shady business. But you can't change your DNA."

"If only I could."

"Is this woman somehow connected to Andrew?" Abigail asked intuitively. She could see that Jasper was deeply troubled. "Is that why you're concerned about her reaction to his being your father?"

Jasper didn't know why he cared about Courtney's reaction to his being Andrew Jackson's son, given the way she'd left him, but he did. Once he made his presence known and swept her back in his arms he would show the princess that she couldn't treat him so cruelly.

"She is," Jasper replied. Seeing the look in his mother's eyes pleading for more information, he returned to the bed. "She is Byron Adams's daughter."

"Oh my God!" Abigail clutched her chest. This had *disaster* written all over it.

"I know, I know." Jasper nodded gloomily.

"How in heaven's name did you meet her?"

"In Punta Cana," Jasper responded. "She was stranded along the road. Her rental car broke down and the rest, as they say, is history."

"And she has no idea who you are?"

Jasper shook his head. "She thinks I'm a construction worker."

"And I take it you didn't disabuse her of that notion?" She arched an eyebrow questioningly.

His mouth curved into a smile. His mother was silent for several long moments and Jasper wondered what she thought of his duplicity.

"You've weaved a dangerous web, son," Abigail said finally. "I just hope it doesn't backfire on you."

Jasper didn't intend it to. He wouldn't allow Courtney Adams to get close enough again for that to happen. This time, he would fire the first shot.

"You didn't have to come with me," Courtney told Gabby as they drove in her Porsche Boxster on the way to the Premiere Atlanta Beauty Show. "You should be in the lab with Shane."

"As much as I love your brother, we don't need to be joined together at the hip every second," Gabrielle said. She was looking forward to her upcoming nuptials, but they already worked in the lab every day and were together at night.

Courtney laughed. "This is true."

When they arrived, the conference center was buzzing. After passing through security and showing their access passes, they were allowed entry. They made their way through the thousands of people from manufacturers to distributors, salon owners to spa professionals, importers to retail buyers to the Adams Cosmetics booth. Several people from their marketing department had already set up the booth and displays, and now it was up to Courtney to draw the crowd over. Once she drew them over, Gabby would explain some of the qualities and effects of their cosmetics and fragrances. The entire family would eventually make their customary appearance, but this was Courtney's baby.

She did notice that Jax Cosmetics was in their same aisle, but farther down. Thank God. Courtney was in no mood for the Jacksons' antics today. She was about business.

"I'm going to go change," Courtney told Gabby, who

was speaking with a marketing representative. If she knew anything about trade shows and conferences, it was that you had to make a splash. She'd brought in her wardrobe bag a black bustier with a jeweled center and a full-length black-and-white polka-dot evening skirt. It would certainly attract attention.

"I'll be here."

Courtney left the trade-show area and was making her way to the restrooms when she ran into Monica Jackson, Andrew Jackson's stepdaughter. Courtney only knew her in passing, and what she knew she didn't like. The petite brunette was always dressed in a pantsuit, and today was no exception. Did she even have an ounce of femininity in her? Her hair was in her usual ponytail, but her makeup was expertly done.

"Well, if isn't little Miss Sunshine," Monica cracked, stepping into Courtney's way.

"Excuse me, Monica," Courtney replied.

"I'm surprised you still bother to come to these events when everyone knows you're washed up," Monica said. "I would think you would be brave enough to allow a young girl to take over. You really are a narcissist. Or maybe you haven't stepped down because your family doesn't trust you to do anything else other than show off your pretty face."

Courtney's eyes flashed with anger. "You don't know the first thing about me."

But what Monica had said had been on the mark. She'd always wondered that herself. Did her family not think her capable of anything else? Sure, they'd listened to her promotional suggestions, but just how open were they to her moving up in AC?

"What I know is you're a self-entitled princess who's had everything handed to her on a silver platter."

"Like you haven't," Courtney responded. She knew that Monica and her mother had done quite well since her mother had married Andrew.

"Maybe now, but my mother and I had to work hard to get what we have."

"Oh yeah? I guess it's hard work trying to snag a millionaire."

Monica took a dangerous step toward her and it was then that Andrew Jackson came forward between them. "Ladies, ladies," he said with a thick country accent. "No reason to allow tempers to flare. We're all here to sell cosmetics and fragrances."

Courtney looked up at Andrew, who towered over her at well over six feet. He was taller than Jasper, Shane and Ethan, but she wasn't intimidated. He was wearing jeans, a suede blazer and a cowboy hat, probably to cover up his slicked-back hair, straight out of the '70s. "Yes, we are," Courtney said, "because some of us can actually create them and not have to steal them. Good day." Courtney turned on her heel and walked quickly away to the restroom.

She hung the garment bag on a partition and paced the restroom floor. She was shaking with rage at Monica's comments and knew she would have to calm down and get in control of her emotions. She shouldn't allow the likes of Monica to get under her skin. Courtney took a few calming breaths through her nose and out of her mouth. After several minutes, she moved inside the stall and opened the wardrobe bag.

When she exited, Courtney was happy with the reflection staring back at her. Her short, honey-blond hair was slicked back so that buyers could focus on her face, which Viola would be making up later during one of the sessions. She added some chandelier earrings, and black studded sandals adorned her feet. She was ready to go and show the Atlanta market once again that Adams Cosmetics was the first choice in cosmetics and fragrances.

Jasper walked through the halls of the convention center in a gray Italian suit. It had a modern fit with notched lapels and a two-button jacket accompanied by matching pants that were comfortable and easy to walk in. He despised wearing suits and was much more comfortable in a pair of old jeans and a T-shirt, but he had to make an impression on Courtney.

He was anxious to see the siren that had walked out on him a week ago without as much as a phone call. He'd shared more with her than he had any other woman, and they were more than compatible in the bedroom. She'd evoked the kind of passion in him that he didn't know he had. He'd thought she'd felt the same as he did, but apparently he was the only one and he felt foolish.

He told himself that seeing her today was just about making her pay for making a fool out of him. He would make her putty in his hands until she was begging him to take her and then walk away, leaving her crushed. But was there more? Was all this just an elaborate ruse so he could see her once more? His mother had warned him that he was playing with fire. But he had to know. He had to know if she would still moan as loud for him as she did in Punta Cana.

He grabbed a layout of the exhibitors and scoured the pages for Adams Cosmetics. He was so determined to find Courtney that he didn't see the man standing in front of him until his name was said aloud.

"Jasper," Andrew Jackson said, "is that really you, son?"

Chapter 9

Jasper sighed wearily. He'd hoped to avoid having a run-in with his father so soon, but luck was not on his side. He glanced up at the old man and saw recognition shine in his eyes.

"Son!" Andrew bent down and wrapped his arms around Jasper's shoulders, which remained still. Andrew stepped back slightly to regard Jasper. His large hands grabbed both sides of his face. "It is you. You look good, boy."

Jasper couldn't say the same for him. He hadn't wanted to lay eyes on his father ever again. He could thank Courtney for this unwelcome reunion. Chasing her had brought him back into Andrew's orbit.

"I'm so happy to see you." Andrew reached for him again to hug him, but Jasper stepped back.

"Don't touch me," Jasper hissed. Andrew had gotten the first hug in because he'd caught him unaware, but he wasn't about to make the same mistake. This was no happy reunion.

"I see you're still angry with me for how I treated your mother," Andrew said, staring down at his son. He could see the hatred shining back in Jasper's eyes.

"You mean the way you bullied her and kept her from her own child?" Jasper said. "Then yes, I still remember. I haven't lost my memory. Or perhaps you have? Are you getting senile in your old age?"

"Now, you listen to me, boy." Andrew's voice rose several pitches, and several people turned around to stare. "I will not have you speak to me that way. I'm still your father. You hear me?"

"Father!" a feminine voice shrieked from behind them.

Jasper stepped away from Andrew and saw Courtney standing behind Andrew. She must have just emerged from the restroom behind them. How long had she been standing there? Had she heard everything?

"This man—" she pointed to Andrew "—is your father?" She blinked with bafflement. She was experiencing a gamut of perplexing emotions as her mind struggled to comprehend all that she'd heard and reconcile it with what she knew. "You're not a construction worker?" She looked at him, disoriented. "You...you're Andrew's long-lost son?"

"Courtney." Jasper went to a make a move toward her, but she held up her hands to ward him off.

"You lied to me!" Her eyes were like polished jade ringed with fire.

Andrew looked at Courtney, then at Jasper. "You know her?"

Jasper didn't answer him. He just started toward Courtney, but she grabbed her skirt, spun around and ran away. "Courtney!" he yelled, but Andrew grabbed his arm.

"How do you know the Adams girl?" Andrew asked again. "I want an answer."

Jasper snatched his arm away. "I don't owe you anything. My life is none of your concern." Seconds later, he was running through the crowd trying to find Courtney. He saw her skirt just as the women's restroom door closed behind her.

"Damn!" Jasper bent over to catch his breath. He hadn't meant for their reunion to be this way. He'd rehearsed it several times in his head, and it certainly shouldn't have started with her discovering he was Andrew Jackson's son.

Courtney paced the restroom floor. Jasper was Andrew's son? She'd fallen in love with the enemy? *Love?* As soon as the words were in her head, Courtney knew them to be true. She was in love with Jasper Jackson. In the short time they'd spent together in Punta Cana, Jasper had captured her heart. In the days since, she'd tried not to think about him, but Tea was right. The problem was she'd fallen for a stone-cold liar.

He'd allowed her to believe he was a construction worker working on a hotel site that was being poorly constructed. Had any of that been true? Or had he just concocted the entire story? Was there anything about the Jasper she'd fallen in love with on the island that was true? Because clearly, she didn't know the real Jasper.

Courtney stayed in the restroom for several minutes hoping that Jasper wasn't outside those doors. She had to pull herself together and get out there for her family; they were depending on her to draw in the crowd to the booth. A wave of apprehension swept through her as she opened the doors and came face-to-face with Jasper.

He was every bit as sexy and handsome as she remembered, except now he was more sophisticated in what she could only surmise was a designer suit. He wore it well.

She moved to the right, but Jasper followed her. When she moved left, he stepped in front of her. "You need to move," she stated emphatically.

"Not until you talk to me."

Courtney looked down at the floor. "I have work to do, now step aside."

"Not until we speak." Jasper grasped Courtney by the arm and walked her out of the hall. She didn't know where he was taking her, but one thing was clear: he wanted the conversation to be private. Eventually, he stopped in front of a set of double doors that led out to a small balcony and guided her through them.

"Don't you dare manhandle me," Courtney said sharply, snatching her arm away. "Not after everything you've done." Her eyes conveyed the fury within her.

Jasper met her accusing eyes, but instead of flinching, he swung her back into the circle of his arms. One hand in the small of her back pressed her forward until their lips was inches apart. "You mean this…?" he said. His lips were urgent and searching as they claimed hers. He forced her lips open with his thrusting tongue and fully explored the recesses of Courtney's mouth. He teased her in ways her body had not forgotten because her breasts began to swell underneath his touch as he caressed them over her bustier. He had said her nipples would remember him, and they did.

Courtney felt her knees weaken and her brain short-circuit. That's when she succumbed to the masterful domination of his lips. She was transported back to another time and place when it had been just her and Jasper lying in the sand on the beach. She could remember his hands sweeping through her hair, caressing her trembling body, but that image also brought her back to reality. It was as if someone had thrown cold water in her face.

She immediately retreated from Jasper, but not before slapping him across the face. He seemed stunned by the action, but didn't make another move toward her.

"I suppose I deserve that," Jasper said.

"You think?" Courtney asked sarcastically.

"But as we both know, you're no angel either, Courtney," Jasper said, rubbing his sore jaw. "*You* walked out on me."

"That was well after you'd been lying to me for weeks," she responded in turn.

Jasper didn't have a quick answer for that.

"You allowed me to believe you were just some lowly construction worker when in actuality you're Andrew Jackson's son!"

Jasper nodded. "You're right. I allowed you to believe I was some poor schmuck, who you obviously felt you could use for kicks. What was your game plan, Courtney? Come down to Punta Cana and have an affair with a local?"

"Don't you turn this around on me, buddy." Courtney poked Jasper in the chest. "Your lies far exceed the way I exited our tryst. If you may recall, you offered me a no-strings-attached affair. I lived up to my end of the bargain."

Jasper was silent. He knew she was right, but clearly somewhere along the line something had changed for the both of them. Neither one of them would be so angry if there were not genuine feelings there.

"But you," Courtney continued her tirade, "led me to believe you were someone you weren't. And now? Now I find out you're the son of my family's *mortal* enemy. This is insane." She ran her fingers through her hair. "What will my family think when they find out?"

"Is that all you care about here? Your family's feelings?" Jasper asked. "What about mine?"

"Did you do this on purpose, Jasper?" Courtney asked, ignoring his question. Tears sprang to her eyes as crazy thoughts spun through her mind. "Did your sleaze of a father send you down to DR to seduce me? Is this his way of getting back at my father, at my family?" She gulped hard as hot tears spilled down her cheeks. "Omigod! I'm an idiot!" Courtney reached for the door to lead her back to the conference hall, but Jasper's large masculine hands closed over hers.

"That isn't what happened, Courtney," Jasper whispered against her ear. "And you know it."

Jasper's nearness made her senses spin and her heart ache. But Courtney couldn't ignore the reality of the situation: she'd been a fool. She'd allowed herself to be used by Andrew's son, but somehow she had to save face and go back in that room for her family. They meant everything to her.

"What I know is that I've never lied to you," she said when she turned to face him. "I've been completely honest with you from the start about who I am. But you…you are a duplicitous liar and I never want to see you again."

Courtney swung open the glass doors and rushed off the balcony. Jasper stared woodenly as the doors closed behind her. His mother was right. He'd played with fire and he'd got burned.

"Are you okay?" Gabrielle asked when Courtney returned to the Adams Cosmetics booth nearly an hour after she'd gone to get dressed. "I thought I was going to have to send a search party out for you."

"I'm fine, I'm fine." Courtney gave a fake smile. "How's everything going?"

"Fine, now that you're here," Ethan said from behind Gabby. "Where have you been?"

Courtney rolled her eyes. Of course, Kayla and Ethan would arrive when she wasn't here. "I'm sorry. I got waylaid by a member of the press," she lied. "You know I'm all about Adams Cosmetics today."

"That's what we need," Kayla said, coming beside her. "You look gorgeous as always." She kissed both of Courtney's cheeks.

"Thanks, love. I'm going to go out and work my magic." Courtney gave them a wave before walking through the crowd. Somehow she managed to put one foot in front of the other and go through the motions of promoting Ecstasy. Several members of the press came over to photograph or interview her. Thanks to the large crowd surrounding her, Courtney was able to lead them back to the Adams Cosmetics booth.

Soon distributors and retailers were swarming their booth. Courtney glanced down the aisle to the Jax Cosmetics booth, which was surprisingly sparse. Monica was standing down the aisle glaring at her, and Courtney gave her a wink. She might be just another pretty face to some, but she knew how to work magic.

"He's Andrew's son?" Tea asked when Courtney begged to come over to her apartment after the trade show. Tea hadn't wanted to because she had a date in a few hours, but at the pleading tone in Courtney's voice she'd relented. She was glad she did. This news was epic. "You're certain?"

"I heard it out of the horse's mouth," Courtney replied. "Andrew called him son."

"Did Jasper deny it?"

"I… We never got around to that," Courtney said testily, jumping up off Tea's couch. "All he wanted to talk about was how I wronged him by leaving without a word."

Tea nodded. "Well, you know I told you he would be sore about that."

"As if that matters now! Not only did he lie about what he did for a living…he lied about who he is at his very core. My God! My father *hates* Andrew Jackson. If he knew I'd slept with his son, much less had feelings for him…" Courtney's voice trailed off.

"Which you do."

Courtney ignored the comment. "This is bad. Real bad. My family can't know about this."

"Do you honestly think you can just sweep this under the rug? You have honest-to-goodness feelings for this man," Tea said. "And if he was willing to come to the trade show to confront you, it means he has feelings for you too. He isn't going to let this go."

Courtney pondered her friend's musings and reluctantly came to sit back on the couch. "Do you really think he cares for me?"

"Why else would he have come?"

"No, no." Courtney shook her head violently. She couldn't allow herself to believe that scenario. "He came here because he'd done his father's bidding and the game was over. He came to rub my face in it and show me how much of a fool I've been."

"Let me ask you something, Courtney," Tea said. "If that's not the case and Jasper came back for you because he wanted to be with you, what then?"

Silence loomed between them. Courtney's stomach churned with anxiety and frustration and, dared she say… hope? The prospect of a relationship with Jasper and her

family's reaction was frightening. She couldn't see or pre-
dict what the outcome would be and that scared her.

"I don't know, Tea."

"How did it go?" his mother asked Jasper when he came
back to the farm later that evening. She was sitting up in
the living room having her usual Earl Grey tea. "Did you
get the closure that you needed?"

"Far from it!" Jasper responded testily. "In fact, I think
I'm more bewildered than ever." Seeing Courtney's reaction to the truth and how devastated she'd been over his de-
ception caused Jasper to realize that perhaps she did have
feelings for him. Had he imagined that? At this point, it
didn't matter because he was still Andrew Jackson's son.
Jasper was certain that if he could have told her the truth
in his own way, they'd be holed up in a hotel room somewhere with Courtney underneath him screaming out his
name after he'd given her a shattering orgasm. And if he
was honest with himself, he doubted he would have been
able to push her away as he'd intended.

"Everything has been turned on its axis," Jasper explained. "Courtney knows who I am now."

"How?"

"I ran into Andrew at the trade show. I thought I'd be
able to avoid him, but he saw me and then Courtney overheard us talking."

"She must be horribly upset with you."

Jasper nodded. "She refuses to speak to me and told me
she never wants to see me again."

"But you don't believe her, I take it?" Abigail asked.

"No, I don't. I don't believe she's being as honest with
herself as I haven't been. Because truth be told, I've fallen
for her, Mama," Jasper replied. "It happened so fast. I
wasn't even looking for it."

"Oh, son, that's wonderful," his mother gushed.

"Not so wonderful, Mama. Her family hates everything Jackson, and that will include me. How will I be able to convince her to give me a second chance?"

Chapter 10

Last night, Jasper had determined that he would have to pull out all the stops to win Courtney back. The problem was she wasn't returning any of his calls. He knew she was angry with him for lying to her about who he was and what he did for a living, but it went deeper.

Courtney had been raised to believe that everything Jackson was wrong, that Andrew Jackson was the devil incarnate. Jasper had heard of Andrew's copying Adams Cosmetics ideas and putting out knockoffs, but the real kicker was that he'd hired Noelle Warner to steal the formula to their new fragrance, Ecstasy.

Jasper could see why Courtney wouldn't want anything to do with the man who was sired by such a criminal. He might be Andrew's offspring, but he prided himself on being nothing like his father. He intended to tell Courtney all of that. But since the mountain wouldn't come to Muhammad, Muhammad would have to come to the mountain.

As he walked into the lobby, a security guard greeted him. "Good morning." He nodded at the burly man. Jasper went to the electronic directory and searched for Courtney's name. He found her on the executive floor and set about righting a wrong.

Courtney was perusing her schedule on her iPad when she noticed a shadow in her peripheral vision and looked up. She stood up, surprised and even more uncertain than she'd been the night before. Why was Jasper here?

"Courtney." Jasper walked inside her office and closed the door behind him. He didn't notice the modern furniture and funky decor of her office. His eyes were only focused on her. She looked smart in a short-sleeve tie-front jacket and wide-legged pants. A large cluster necklace was around her swanlike neck, and several bangles were on her arm. Courtney was the picture of sophistication and looked nothing like the sexy free spirit in a tank and shorts he'd met in Punta Cana.

"What are you doing here?" Courtney asked.

"I'm here to have my say," Jasper replied. "Yesterday, you had your turn and today is mine."

"In case you hadn't noticed—" Courtney swept her arms around "—this is a place of business, not a place to air our dirty laundry."

"If you'd returned my calls yesterday, we could have done this elsewhere, but since you didn't…" He shrugged. "I'm here."

"Nothing you can say will change anything."

Jasper's eyes traveled over her face and searched her jade eyes. She was lying. "I beg to differ. Hear me out first, and if you still don't believe me, I will leave you alone."

Courtney raised one perfectly arched eyebrow. She

doubted it. She went to sit down at her desk, but Jasper asked, "Can we sit on the couch?"

She opened her mouth to protest, but figured the sooner they got this over with, the better. Reluctantly, she walked toward the couch, but sat as far as possible on the opposite end. Of course, she hadn't counted on the intoxicating smell of his cologne or the pull she felt whenever she was around him. It was undeniable. Whenever he was around, there was a tingling in the pit of her stomach. She folded her hands in her lap and tried to calm her nerves. She had no intention of permitting herself to fall under his spell again, not after all his lies.

"My name is Jasper Jackson," he began, "and yes, I am Andrew Jackson's son, but I have no relationship with the man."

He looked at Courtney to see if she was still with him, but her face was emotionless, so he continued. "My father was a cold, heartless man who married my mother only after he'd learned your mother had married another man."

That generated a reaction. "Oh…" Courtney's hand flew to her mouth, and Jasper knew he had her attention.

"Andrew met my mother, Abigail, the night he found out Elizabeth had married your father, Byron Adams. He used Abigail, and only when he discovered she was pregnant did he agree to marry her with the hopes she would have a son. Lucky for him, she did. Otherwise he would have thrown her out sooner. He didn't love my mother and shut her out. She was just a poor farm girl who had no place in society. My mother tried to be a good wife to the bastard, but he was a miserable man. When I was seven, she ran away and tried to take me with her to my grandfather's farm, but Andrew used his lawyers to intimidate her and get me back."

"That's awful." Courtney couldn't imagine being separated from her mother at such a young age.

"After that, she was only allowed to see me when Andrew saw fit, which wasn't often. I hated him and vowed to return to my mother one day. When I was fifteen, I became legally emancipated and went to live with my mother."

"I'm sure Andrew didn't like that very much."

"No, he didn't, but he didn't have much choice. I blackmailed him with the knowledge I had about his shady business dealings. You see, I was smart and listened in on his conversations. Knowing I could out him, Andrew let me go."

"You blackmailed your own father?" She regarded him with somber curiosity. Who did such a thing? Did she even know this man?

Jasper nodded. "I had to and I don't regret it. Going to live with my mother was the best thing that could have happened to me. I learned how to till the land from my grandfather and become a craftsman like my uncle by working for his construction company. He showed me how to work with my hands and build things. I went on to college and became an architect. I always had a vision of being an entrepreneur, so I convinced the bank and some investors to back me on my first hotel. One hotel led to another and so on."

"So you do know about construction?" Courtney asked aloud. She was trying to put all the pieces together. "So that much wasn't a lie."

"It wasn't all a lie, Courtney. I was concerned about the company constructing my second hotel in Punta Cana and went undercover as a construction worker to find out what was going on, and when I did, I fired the company. The lie was that I owned the hotel being constructed and Sea Breeze Resorts as well."

Her thoughts filtered back to the hotel manager and several other people around the town and how they'd catered to Jasper's every need. "So Miguel and your entire staff were in on your lie?"

"I asked them for their discretion," Jasper answered honestly.

"I see." Courtney's fingers tensed in her lap and her voice broke slightly when she asked, "And what do you want from me now?"

"I want you to forgive me," Jasper responded.

"Why?"

"Because I want you in my life. I need you in my life."

Courtney's breath caught in her lungs and she stared at him speechless.

"I know I deceived you about who I was," Jasper said, scooting closer to her on the couch until they were inches apart. "I was wrong. I offered you a no-strings-attached affair because that's all I thought I had to give, but when I met you that changed. We connected like I never had with anyone before. I was upset that you left me because in a short span of time I've come to care for you deeply."

Courtney's eyes became clouded with tears and she bit her lip, trying to hold herself in check. "This can't work, Jasper." She swiftly rose from the couch. "I think you should go." She turned her back to him and faced the window.

Courtney's resolve weakened when he walked toward her and stood behind her. "It would be a bitter price to pay if we allowed our parents to come between us."

Jasper's strong, muscular arms encircled her slim waist, and a tear trickled down her cheek as her body tingled from the contact. How could she give him up? But if she didn't, it would be insanity. But her heart... She turned around to face him, and Jasper's large hands cupped her face.

"Baby, I know you have your doubts, but I believe we can work this out—" His lips came down on hers, and warmth rushed through her. She tilted her head and it fit perfectly in the hollow between his shoulder and neck. The kiss sent spirals of ecstasy shooting through her. She gave herself freely to the passion of his kiss and fused her mouth and tongue with his.

She didn't hear her office door open, until she heard "What the hell?"

Courtney jumped back when she heard her sister's voice and turned to face her.

"So it's true," Kayla said.

Courtney looked up, disoriented. "What's true?"

"This!" Kayla held up the gossip section of a local tabloid that had a large color picture of Courtney and Jasper kissing outside on the balcony at the trade show.

Courtney was thrown. "*Who* took that?"

"Who do you think?" Fury raged inside Kayla. "Probably him or his scum of a father." Kayla pointed to Jasper.

Jasper held up his hands. "I had nothing to do with that."

"Of course you didn't," Kayla replied shortly. "What the hell is going on, Courtney? You were supposed to be getting us positive press about Ecstasy and instead you're caught in a lip lock with Andrew Jackson's son of all people? For Christ's sake, what is going on with you?"

"Kayla, this isn't what you think."

"You don't have to explain our relationship to her," Jasper said, from her side. "This is between me and you. Not your family."

Courtney turned to glare at Jasper before addressing her sister. "There is a lot you don't understand, and I would be happy to explain it to you once you've calmed down."

"Just as well, because I've called a family meeting," Kayla said, throwing down the tabloid as she left. "I will see you after work, and don't be late. Otherwise, Dad might have to go looking for you with a shotgun like he did when you were eighteen and ran off with Chaise."

Seconds later, Kayla had departed, leaving Jasper and Courtney alone.

"Wow!" Jasper stepped back. "Is she always that intense?"

"Not usually," Courtney replied, anxiously rubbing her hands together. "But her reaction will be nothing compared to my father's when he finds out about us."

"What could really happen?" Jasper asked, trying to be lighthearted.

"You remember that shotgun Kayla mentioned?" Courtney said, looking up at him intently. "She wasn't joking."

Jasper swallowed hard.

"What did you just say?" Byron Adams asked his eldest when she and Ethan came over to the estate for a family meeting. Kayla had been cryptic over the phone, and that had put Byron instantly on edge. Whenever she sounded that way, he knew the news wasn't good, like when she'd told them Adams Cosmetics was merging with Graham International. So he was prepared to hear something unpleasant, but this was unthinkable.

"I said that Courtney is involved with Andrew Jackson's son, Jasper."

"Like hell!" Byron roared. "Where is he?" He moved toward the door. "I will put a bullet in that young man before the night's out for touching my daughter."

Elizabeth Adams rose from her chair to stop her irrational husband. "Byron, please. Don't get yourself this upset, you'll have a heart attack."

"I'm having one, Lizzie," he said, calling her by the nickname he only used when it was just the two of them.

"Our *daughter* is involved with Andrew's son. Of all people, she had to get herself messed up with him. What the hell is she thinking?"

"I don't think she was thinking," Shane joked.

"Shane!" his mother admonished.

"What?" Shane shrugged. "We all know Courtney is a free spirit and lives life on her own terms. Why should this be any different?"

Kayla was surprised by Shane's response given what Andrew Jackson had done to his fiancée, Gabrielle, by attempting to blackmail her and steal his fragrance. "How can you joke about this, Shane? You of all people know that Andrew can't be trusted. He's a liar and a thief, and no doubt Jasper Jackson is cut from the same cloth."

"I'm with Shane on this one. I believe you all thought the same thing about me at some point, but I'm nothing like Carter," said Ethan, referring to his father.

Byron said jokingly, "I wouldn't say that...."

Ethan glared at his father-in-law. "All I'm saying is we should give the guy a chance before you crucify him."

"I would agree," Courtney said from behind Ethan.

Ethan stepped aside so she could walk into the center of the family room where everyone was gathered discussing her love life.

"In heaven's name, child, what possessed you to get involved with Andrew's son?" her mother asked. She wanted to be the voice of reason, but even she couldn't understand why Courtney would knowingly cause this kind of friction in the family.

"I didn't know who he was."

"Courtney..." Kayla sighed. "So you just got involved with some strange man without finding out who he was."

When her sister put it like that, it made Courtney look

like a hussy in front of her father and brother. Courtney lowered her head, completely embarrassed.

Kayla apologized immediately. "I'm sorry, that sounded harsh. Where did you meet him?"

"In Punta Cana."

"So he followed you down there?" her father asked. "I wouldn't put it past Andrew to keep tails on all of us."

"It wasn't like that, Daddy," Courtney replied. "Jasper owns Sea Breeze Resorts."

"The Sea Breeze Resorts where Gabby and I stayed?" Shane asked.

"The one and the same." Courtney nodded. "Jasper is estranged from Andrew. He's had no dealings with him since he was fifteen years old because Andrew kept him from his mother."

Byron snorted. "Why am I not surprised?"

Courtney continued, "After he was fifteen he stayed with his mother on a farm in Marietta and then built a hotel empire on his own without a dime from his father. Daddy—" Courtney walked over to her father and searched his face "—even you must respect that. He's tried to distance himself from Andrew's underhanded business."

"He's still a Jackson," Byron stated.

Courtney swallowed. She knew it wasn't going to be easy convincing her family of Jasper's sincerity. It was going to be an uphill battle.

"If Courtney isn't serious about this young man," her mother said, "this could be a moot point. I mean, I know you like your freedom, my dear. But I can't imagine you continuing this dalliance."

All eyes in the room turned to stare at Courtney and she stiffened, momentarily abashed. She felt as if she were onstage with a gigantic spotlight on her. She hadn't had time to analyze her feelings for Jasper and digest all the information he'd given her, much less share her feelings for him with her family.

So she answered as honestly as she could. "I don't know."

"What do you mean, you don't know?" Her father glared at her. A warning cloud settled on his features. "Are you telling me you're in love with this young man?"

Courtney's cheeks burned and her breath quickened. "It means I don't know, Daddy. It's too soon for me to know what my feelings are after a couple of weeks, but I can tell you that I intend to explore them."

"Excuse me?"

Courtney hated going up against her father, but this was one of those defining moments in her life where she knew she had to make a stand whether he liked what she had to say or not. "I have feelings for Jasper," she stated very clearly so there was no misunderstanding of her intent. "And I know he's Andrew Jackson's son, but I don't care. Just because he was raised under his roof doesn't mean he's like his father. C'mon, Kayla."

She looked to her sister with imploring eyes. They'd always shared a bond; surely she would understand. "You've been in my shoes. Everyone thought Ethan—" she pointed to her brother-in-law "—was like his father, but he wasn't."

"That's different," Kayla said, coming toward her sister and grasping her by the shoulders. "We all grew up with Ethan. We know nothing about this Jasper. How can we be sure we can trust him? How do we know this isn't an elaborate ruse that he and Andrew have concocted to annihilate our family? That's been his goal for decades."

"We don't know," Courtney replied, disengaging Kayla's hands from her shoulders and turning to face the family. "I guess for once you're all just going to have to trust my judgment." *Here is their opportunity to show that they*

*believe in and respect me and don't think that I'm some
flighty airhead they have to watch over.*

"This doesn't just affect you, baby girl," their father replied stiffly. "This affects the entire family. Because it's personal. Andrew has made it personal."

"It doesn't have to be that way, Daddy," Courtney said. "You can *choose* to give Jasper the benefit of the doubt. This is about me and Jasper and nothing more. *You're* turning it into business."

"Courtney…" Her father towered over her and said firmly, "You need to do what's right and end this affair, right now."

"I'm not eighteen years old, Daddy," she said, looking up at him. "You can't just tell me what to do anymore and think I'm going to roll over like a good little puppy dog. I'm a grown woman and I know what I want and I want Jasper."

"He comes from a clan of liars and thieves, and I forbid you to see him!"

"I'm warning you, Daddy," Courtney said loudly. The words sounded strange on her tongue, but she said them anyway. "Don't make me choose. You may not like my choice."

Her father frowned with cold fury. "Don't you speak to me in that tone!"

Kayla could see their father's blood pressure rising. "Daddy, I think it's best if we table this discussion." She came and stood between the two of them. The tension emanating from them both was coming off in droves.

"Kayla's right," their mother said. "I think it's best we all go our separate ways for the evening. Byron." She rose and walked over to grasp her husband's hand. "I would like to speak with you privately, please."

After her parents had gone, Kayla and Ethan weren't

far behind. "We'll talk later." She stiffly kissed Courtney's cheek before departing, leaving Courtney and Shane
alone in the room.

"Wow!" Shane clapped loudly.

"What's that for?" Courtney asked.

"I didn't think you had it in you, little sis," Shane replied, walking over to the wet bar to pour himself a glass
of vodka on the rocks and another for Courtney, but adding cranberry juice for her. When he was done, he handed
her a glass.

"Thanks." Courtney took a generous gulp.

"Easy, now." Shane smiled as he watched her.

Reluctantly, Courtney smiled as well. "I needed that.
Now, what didn't you think I could do?"

"Stand up to Dad. He can be pretty intimidating."

"Trust me, it wasn't easy. I almost peed in my pants."
Courtney laughed nervously. "But I can't let him walk
all over me. He may have been right when I was eighteen
about my quickie marriage to Chaise, but he's not right
about Jasper. Jasper's different from any other man I've
been with. He makes me feel safe."

Shane nodded quietly and sipped on his drink.

"You surprised me too," Courtney said. "Given your
animosity toward Andrew Jackson, I just knew you would
be against this relationship."

"I don't trust the guy," Shane said. After everything Andrew had done to Gabby, he was concerned. "But I trust
you and if you say Jasper's worth it, then I'll try and get
along with him, the same as I did with Ethan. But he'll
have to earn my trust."

Courtney smiled at her older brother. "Thank you,
Shane. That means a lot."

Chapter 11

Jasper was anxious as he waited for Courtney at the Hyatt Regency hotel, where he'd reserved a suite. He'd driven up the night before from the farm because he was determined to make Courtney listen to him. He'd hoped that once he got her alone, she would listen to him and he could tell her his past. She had. She'd kept an open mind and one thing had led to another, and they'd shared another kiss. A kiss that had transported him back to Punta Cana when he'd been lying wrapped up in her arms. It was the closest to heaven he'd ever gotten.

And now he hoped that Courtney would give him a chance to make things right. He'd asked her to come to his hotel so they could talk, and he hoped she would. He knew it was a lot to ask given that he'd deceived her, but he was hoping that her feelings for him outweighed her anger. It was funny that he'd come back to the States intent on making Courtney pay for a perceived wrong, and instead he'd realized that he didn't want to let her go.

Courtney drove her Porsche Boxster to the Hyatt Regency, even got out of the car and handed her keys to the valet, but then she chickened out of going upstairs to Jasper's room and instead headed to the bar for a drink.

It had been a tough night. She'd never spoken that way to her father. She'd always just done as he told her. Although Jasper had lied to her about who he was and what he did for a living, for some reason she just wasn't ready for what they shared to end. And she certainly was going to allow her father to bully her. She was capable of making her own decisions.

She'd been hurt that Kayla hadn't backed her up on her decision to continue seeing Jasper. Courtney hadn't been happy when Kayla had married Ethan, but she'd stood by her when she too had encountered their father's wrath. Where was the sisterly unity? She was going to have a few words with her older sister.

Yet she was afraid to go forward with Jasper. If she went upstairs to his suite, Jasper would think he'd won and try to take her to bed, and with his lips on hers, Courtney's defenses might weaken and she would let him. Then he would think it was okay for him to lie to her and get away with it. And that she couldn't abide.

As she sipped her scotch, Courtney thought about what to do. The problem was she wanted to give Jasper the benefit of the doubt and believe that he'd made a bad judgment call that had spiraled out of control. Given the weeks they'd spent together, Courtney couldn't believe the absolute worst about him. There was some good in Jasper. She'd seen it for herself in how he cared for those orphan children or how he wanted the best for his workers. She just had to reconcile the two together.

After an hour, Jasper became nervous. Courtney had called him after she'd left her family's estate and told him she would be there within the hour. Had she changed her mind and decided not to come?

He checked his cell phone, and there was no voice mail or text message, so he checked with the front desk just in case she had called the hotel. He rushed over to the nightstand and picked up the receiver. "Are there any messages for me?" he inquired. "From Courtney Adams."

"Ms. Adams?" the front desk clerk asked. "There are no messages, but she arrived about half an hour ago."

"She did?" Where was she?

"Yes, she's in the bar, I believe."

"Thank you." Jasper quickly replaced the receiver and, grabbing the hotel key card, left the room. He knew that she hadn't come all this way for nothing. Clearly, she was conflicted about seeing him, but at least she hadn't left. Jasper took that as a good sign. A short elevator ride later, he was walking through the lobby. He could hear the mellow croons of a chanteuse at the piano bar.

The bar was partially crowded, with several people in business attire sitting at smaller tables surrounding the piano and a long, circular bar where various liquors hung from the rafters.

Jasper found Courtney at the bar, nursing a glass of scotch. She'd changed out of the suit she was wearing earlier and was wearing jeans and a sweater with boots. "Care if I join you?" he asked.

Courtney hazarded a glance in his direction. "Don't mind if you do." She returned her gaze to the bottom of the glass.

"It went that bad?" Jasper asked, sliding his barstool closer to her. "I'll have the same thing she's having," he told the bartender who'd come up. He knew that Courtney's family wouldn't be too happy after her sister had walked in on them making out in her office.

"Worse!" Courtney downed the rest of her drink and slid the glass down the bar. "Bartender, another please."

"Hmm…how many of those have you had?" Jasper asked. When she didn't respond, he motioned to the bartender to cut her off after that drink. "So, what happened?"

"If you can believe it, my father forbade me, a twenty-seven-year-old woman, to see you. Thank you." She accepted the drink from the bartender and took a quick sip.

"He forbade you?"

"Yes. Can you believe that?" She chuckled, clearly amused by the word. "You would think we were back in ancient times or something."

"What did you tell him?" Jasper asked.

"I told him not to make me choose because he may not like my decision."

"Wow!" Jasper whirled around on the barstool to stare at Courtney. The woman had chutzpah. "And how did he take that?"

"Not well."

"I'm sorry," Jasper said. "I don't want to cause discord between you and your family."

"Well, perhaps you should have thought of that before you lied to me about who you were," she said crisply.

"You're right. I should have told you." He took a swig of scotch. "But instead I was focused on what I wanted, which is you."

Courtney eyed him suspiciously.

"If you knew who I was related to, would you have stayed with me in Punta Cana?" Jasper asked.

Courtney paused to think about his question. She finally answered, "No, I wouldn't have. Had I known you were Andrew Jackson's son, I would not have given you a second glance."

"Even though I have no relationship with the man?"

"Even then."

"I appreciate your honesty," Jasper said, "but I am who I am and I can't change who my father is. Though I wish I could. So I guess you have to decide if that's a deal breaker or not. You've indicated to your family that they wouldn't like your decision, but I'm still in the dark. Will my bloodline exclude me from being your man?"

"Is that what you want to be?" Courtney asked. He noticed that she seemed to be holding her breath as she waited for his response.

"If you'll let me."

From the expression on her face, Jasper could tell that a war of emotions raged inside Courtney. He knew that she didn't relish being at odds with her family, but she also couldn't deny that Jasper had touched something deep inside her. He just hoped she would want to explore it.

Jasper's stomach clenched tightly as he waited for her answer. "Well?"

"There will be time to figure out the particulars later," Courtney said. She placed her drink on the bar and rose from her stool. "Let's go upstairs."

Once in his suite, although Jasper desired her, he found himself feeling oddly protective of her. She was putting herself at great odds for the privilege of being with him, and he didn't want her to think that he only cared about her body and nothing else. He cared about her well-being too.

He helped her to the bed and then knelt to unzip and pull off her boots. She seemed surprised that he was taking care of her. She probably suspected that he would take her to bed because the passion they'd shared in Punta Cana had been off the charts, but he wanted Courtney to know that there was more to him than being her lover.

"Thanks," she said when he removed one calf-length boot and then the other. She rose for Jasper to undress her, but instead he walked away and went to the open suitcase on the floor.

He removed an oversize T-shirt from the suitcase and brought it toward her.

"What's that for?"

"For you to sleep in."

"You mean, we're not gonna…you know." She winked as she came toward him, but ended up stumbling slightly into his arms. "Gonna do it?"

Jasper grasped her under her arms before she fell. "There will be time for that another night." He righted her so he could pull the sweater she wore over her head and throw it across a nearby chair. Then he pulled the oversize T-shirt over her head. Her skintight jeans were next; he unzipped them with ease and slid them down her legs. She stepped out of them and he threw them over the sweater.

"Come to bed, baby," Jasper crooned, pulling the large damask comforter back and settling Courtney between the cool, crisp white linens and down pillows.

"Aren't you joining me?" Courtney asked when Jasper left her side.

Jasper smiled. "Yes, but no hanky-panky." He removed his trousers and shirt, leaving him in only his undershirt and boxers, and then joined her inside the bed.

He pulled her into the safety of his arms and Courtney came willingly. She nestled her head in the crook underneath his neck and rested her face against his chest. With Courtney so close, Jasper could feel her nipples pucker underneath the thin T-shirt she wore. Despite the desires of the lower half of his body, Jasper focused on just being there for Courtney. He kissed her head and lightly stroked her hair.

"Thank you," she murmured against his chest as she curled into the curve of his body. "I think I needed *this* more than sex."

"I know," Jasper said as he leaned over to turn off the light on the nightstand. "Sleep and we'll talk in the morning."

In the morning light, everything was crystal clear to Courtney. She knew she'd made the right decision in choosing Jasper. He'd shown her last night that their relationship could be about more than just mutual gratification. It could be about caring and comfort. It was the first time she'd allowed a man to get this close, and she was no worse for the wear for doing so. Perhaps Kayla and Shane had it right about finding someone that completed you.

"Good morning, beautiful," Jasper whispered against her ear when she woke up.

Courtney glanced up and found Jasper was up and watching her.

"You have an intent look on your face," Jasper said. "I hope you're not regretting your decision to give me another chance."

Courtney shook her head. "I'm not. I trust my gut instinct."

Jasper smiled and his eyes contained a sensual flame. "I'm glad to hear that." He lowered his head to give her a slow, shivery kiss that caused desire to burn within her. She wrapped her arms around his neck and pulled him firmly against her. There would be time for talking later. She'd been emotional and a little bit tipsy last night, but she was awake now and aching for the fulfillment of his lovemaking. Jasper did not disappoint.

* * *

"Shane told me about what happened last night," Gabrielle said from outside the dressing room. When Courtney arrived at the bridal shop to pick up the bridesmaid dresses after they'd been altered, she was surprised to find it was just the two of them. Apparently, Gabby had purposely told Kayla and Courtney's mother to arrive thirty minutes later so she would have time to talk to her dear friend and soon-to-be sister-in-law. Gabby's other bridesmaid, Mariah, lived in Paris, so she had had her dress shipped to Paris's best alteration seamstress and would bring it with her when she flew in for the wedding.

"Yeah, the family—rather my Dad and Kayla—aren't too happy with my dating choices these days," Courtney replied from inside the dressing room as she fastened the strapless bra she intended to wear underneath the champagne-colored dress. She pulled the dress over her head and admired herself in the mirror. She looked pretty good for a bridesmaid, she thought. She came out of the dressing room so Gabby could see.

"It looks great," Gabrielle said, adjusting the bosom of the dress ever so slightly. Courtney had a smaller chest and was not as full figured as Kayla had become since Alexander's birth and breast-feeding. "What do you think?"

Courtney turned so she could see the back in the three-way mirror. "Looks good to me."

Gabrielle reached for both of Courtney's hands and pulled her to the nearby ottoman. "And how are you handling things?" she inquired. "Your family is *so* close. I can't imagine you at odds."

"Neither can I," Courtney answered honestly. "And I don't want to cause any disruption to your wedding festivities as they draw closer, but I won't let Daddy bully me either. He actually forbade me to see Jasper like I was some naive teenager."

"So I heard, but you're going to continue dating him, right?"

Courtney nodded. "I am. And no one's going to stop me."

Gabrielle smiled broadly. "Good for you. I want you to be as happy as Shane and I are, because if you hadn't given me a shove and helped me admit my feelings for your brother, I would still be alone and unhappy." Her almond-shaped brown eyes misted with tears. "I have you to thank for my new life."

"I'm so tickled that you're going to be part of my family, I could just burst." Courtney smiled, squeezing Gabby's hand.

"So are we," Elizabeth and Kayla said in unison from behind the duo. Startled, they both guiltily raised their heads as if they'd been caught in a clandestine conversation.

Gabrielle rose from the ottoman and gave Elizabeth a hug. "So happy you guys could make it. Your dresses are all here and ready for you to try on." She motioned to the two dresses hanging next to her wedding gown, which she had been waiting to try on until everyone had arrived.

"Did we get the time wrong?" Kayla asked, glancing at her sister, who was already in her bridesmaid's dress.

Gabrielle shook her head. "No. Courtney and I just needed some alone time. Come." She grasped Kayla's arm and pulled her toward the rack.

While they talked, her mother came toward Courtney. "How are you, my darling?" she asked, tucking a wayward strand of Courtney's hair behind her ear. "You didn't sleep at home last night."

"You noticed."

"You're my daughter. Of course I notice these things," Elizabeth replied. "It's why I want to talk to you. Your father behaved insufferably last night and I'm truly sorry about that. I've told him he must apologize at once."

Courtney wasn't surprised by her mother's blunt talk; she had a way of wrapping her father around her little finger. "Mama, I appreciate that, but you know that won't change anything. Daddy's never going to accept my dating Andrew's son."

"He will have to learn," Elizabeth stated. "I think you should invite Jasper to dinner with the family."

"I don't think that's a wise idea, Mama. I think it will only cause chaos."

"I will not have discord in the family and most certainly not because of Andrew. He's hurt my family enough. Matter of fact, I have a mind to go and talk to him. Give him a piece of my mind."

"No, no." Courtney shook her head. "That will only infuriate Daddy. You know he doesn't even like you near that man. Please just stay out of this."

"I know," Elizabeth said regretfully, "it's just that I feel so helpless. I feel like it's my fault that Andrew keeps attacking our family. All because of what happened decades ago."

"It's not your fault, Mama. And you certainly can't control that I met and fell for Jasper's son."

"Are you saying you love him?" Her mother's eyes grew large.

Courtney wasn't ready to admit to herself or her mother that it was love. She doubted she'd ever been in love. Lust, she understood. It was just an animal attraction, but love was another matter entirely. "It has the makings of being serious," she replied instead.

Elizabeth noticed that her youngest daughter chose her

words very carefully. "Hmm…well, sometimes love happens rather quickly. Then again, sometimes it happens over time."

"Is that how it was with you and Daddy?" Courtney asked.

"Yes, it was slow and gradual. As Andrew and I drifted further apart, Byron and I grew closer. And in time, friendship turned into love."

"I think Jasper and I kind of did it backward," Courtney said. "We were hot and heavy at the start, and now I think we could learn a thing or two from you about being friends."

Elizabeth smiled. "Thirty-six years of marriage and still counting…."

"And that's my hope for Shane and me," Gabrielle said, joining the duo with a big smile on her face, "that we can be nearly as happy as you and Mr. Adams have been all these years."

"We have no doubt you will be," Elizabeth said cheerily.

Chapter 12

"Son, you don't have to help with the chores," Abigail Jackson told Jasper a couple of days later when he stopped by to check in on her.

"I know, Mama," Jasper replied, setting the tray of tea and sandwiches on her nightstand. "But I offered to help, so it's no problem."

"I doubt cleaning out the stables is much fun for you," she responded. "I can't remember the last time you got your hands dirty." Once he'd become successful with his hotel business, Jasper had hired some ranch hands to help her with the farm.

"Well, actually, the last time was a month ago when I met Courtney."

"Oh, yes." She chuckled. "When you pretended to be a construction worker."

"It wasn't a far stretch." Jasper laughed with her. "Working summers with Uncle Duke wasn't easy either."

"Ah, but think about all the practical knowledge you obtained. Helped you become a brilliant architect and start your own business."

"I wouldn't say brilliant, but you're right. I wouldn't be where I am today without it."

"And that's a good place?" Her voice sounded hopeful.

Jasper smiled. "Yes, the hotel business is going great and Courtney...well, we're moving in the right direction."

"Does that mean I'm going to see more of you from now on?" she asked.

Jasper nodded. "Most definitely. Listen, I'm going to go finish up, but I'll see you in a bit. Eat up." He inclined his head to the turkey sandwich and tomato soup.

He left the room and bounded down the old wooden stairs, intent on cleaning out the stables and adding some fresh hay and such. He swung open the front door and was surprised to find his father standing on the porch.

Jasper sighed wearily. And he was having such a good day, he thought to himself. "What do you want, Andrew?" He pushed past him so they were standing outside. He didn't want his mother to get upset and overhear the conversation. Of course, just having Andrew on her property was probably enough to do that.

"I came to see my long-lost son," Andrew replied, "since you obviously didn't have any intention of coming to see me."

"I told you when I left that house that I would never return. I haven't changed my mind."

"Jasper, son." Andrew touched Jasper's arm. "Don't you think it's time we let bygones be bygones? What happened between your mother and me was a long time ago. I'm sure she's forgiven me by now. Why can't you?"

"Forgiven you?" Jasper said ruefully. "I highly doubt that. She despises you as I do."

Hurt etched across Andrew's face at Jasper's harsh words. "You can't mean that," he said. "I've never harmed you. You were given the best I had to offer. You had the best clothes and toys, the finest education..."

"But I didn't have *my mother*," Jasper responded. "You saw to that."

"Abigail didn't belong in my world. And she knew it. It was why she left us, left you."

Jasper pointed a finger at him. "Don't you dare rewrite history, Andrew! My mother didn't *leave me!* She left *you* because you gave her no choice. You were hung up on Elizabeth Adams. Heck, you still are."

"You're wrong about that. In case you hadn't noticed or heard, I remarried. Blythe and I are quite happy."

"Is that a fact?" Jasper laughed.

"Don't you mock me, boy!"

"And don't you play me for a fool," Jasper responded. "If you didn't still love Courtney's mother, you wouldn't have started Jax Cosmetics. And you wouldn't be constantly trying to one-up Byron Adams and his family to prove to Elizabeth that she made the wrong choice."

"You have no idea what you're talking about," Andrew said, pacing the porch. But Jasper could see he'd hit the nail on the head.

"Does the truth hit a little too close to home for you, *Dad?* I think it's about time someone showed you a mirror and who you've become. You've spent your entire life living in another man's shadow. Have you no pride, no self-respect? Get on with your life. Accept the fact that you will *never* get her back."

"She was my first love!" Andrew yelled. "You have no idea what it's been like all these years, watching her marry *my best friend,* bear his children, start a company with him."

Jasper stared back at Andrew, stunned by the revelation. It was probably the first honest moment he'd ever had with his father.

"I loved that woman," Andrew stated wearily. "I loved her more than any other woman before her or since."

That Jasper knew. His mother had known Andrew didn't love her. He'd merely married her because she was carrying his son, his heir.

"It was my greatest regret that I let her slip away, that I allowed Byron to sneak his way into her heart. I blame myself. I have for years. I had the best woman in the world, but I was too selfish to know it back then."

"If you know this, why don't you just let this vendetta you have against the Adams family go?"

"I can't and I won't." His father shook his head. "Byron deserves to pay for what he did to me. He was supposed to be *my* friend, but instead he went behind my back and took my woman. The only way I can repay him is to attack the one thing he loves more than Elizabeth or his brood, his company. I know that's the one thing I can take away from him that will make him hurt the most."

Jasper was surprised that he actually felt pity for the old man. He was holding on to a grudge that had cost him his pride, dignity, self-respect and ultimately his son. "I'm sorry to hear you say that. I know you're a smart man, but you must know that going against Adams Cosmetics, which is helmed by Elizabeth's children, would hurt the lady herself. You know that this will not bring her back and she will despise you."

His father's eyes turned to stone. "I realize that. And so be it. If I can't have her, I will destroy Adams Cosmetics. And you're in a prime position to help me. With your newfound relationship with the Adams girl, you could get me the intel I need for payback. It's time you accepted your place in this family."

Jasper laughed at his father's delusions. "You're just as sick and twisted as I remember." He shook his head in amazement. "If you think I'd ever move a finger to help you, you have another thought coming. After what you did to me? To my mother?"

"Ah yes, your mother." Andrew looked up to the second floor and laughed devilishly. "I heard she had an untimely fall."

Jasper watched his father and noticed the glee in his voice at his mother's situation and cringed inwardly. "How can you get satisfaction from someone else's distress?" Jasper was horrified. "Get off this land and never come near me or my mother again."

"I'll leave when I'm good and ready to," Andrew said, walking toward him and towering over Jasper. "You may be young and strong, but I can still take you, boy."

"I don't doubt you can, but listen to me, because I'm telling you this for the last and final time." Jasper looked up at his father. "I want nothing to do with you, your little schemes or Jax Cosmetics. I want nothing from you."

"Then I will disown you," Andrew stated without missing a beat, "give the money to your stepsister, Monica."

Jasper shrugged. "Be my guest. She's been more of a son to you than I've ever been." From what he'd heard, Monica Jackson was desperate for his father's approval and had no conscience. She would do whatever was necessary to win his praise.

His father glared at him, but Jasper could see behind the glare that he was shaken. He probably assumed that at some point Jasper would get over his anger toward him and eventually rejoin the fold, but he was wrong. Jasper had never felt as though he belonged in Jackson Manor or in his father's world. He was happier here with his mother on the farm, as he'd always been.

"Do as you wish," Andrew said, "but know this. If you're not with me, you're against me. And as your mother knows, I take no prisoners." He sauntered off the porch steps and strode toward the limousine that was waiting for him down the path.

A strange sense of dread washed over Jasper because he believed every word that had come out of his father's mouth. His father now considered him an enemy, which made the situation very dangerous indeed.

Courtney wasn't happy when Jasper told her he had to make a return trip to Punta Cana before his first Adams family dinner. He'd had to get back to meet with the second bidder who'd come in after Dorchester Construction. Jasper was trying to get them in place so he could rest easy during Shane and Gabrielle's wedding festivities. Of course, it meant she would have no time to prepare him for meeting her family. It was going to be a trial by fire.

As she walked into Kayla's office, Courtney suspected she was not going to be a stranger to trial by fire. They were meeting to discuss Courtney expanding her role at the company. It had been nearly a week since they'd last spoken, which had given them enough space to calm down. However, Courtney knew that the topic of conversation would eventually stray to her boyfriend. But that was okay, because Courtney had a bone to pick with Kayla as well about her reaction to Jasper.

To show her new mature side, Courtney had dressed in a winter-white boatneck dress and bolero jacket. Although she'd toned down her look, she was still fashionably chic.

Her older sister was waiting for her in her office, dressed in a brown multicolored tweed skirt suit that belied her age. Sometimes Courtney wished Kayla was not so stiff, but she knew that she had to dress the part for her position.

"You wanted to see me?" Courtney asked from the doorway.

Kayla smiled and motioned her in. "Yes, come in."

Closing the door, Courtney walked toward Kayla, who'd come from behind her desk to greet her. They exchanged a customary quick kiss on the cheeks and Courtney followed Kayla's lead by going to the couch in her office and taking a seat.

"I want you to know that I've listened to you and I've heard your concerns," Kayla began. "You're restless. You want to be more than a spokesmodel. You want a say in the marketing strategy for Adams Cosmetics."

"All of the above," Courtney said. "I'm twenty-seven and I've had a great run, but it's time I retired and we find a new spokesmodel. But I would like to be part of the decision-making process for my replacement."

"Absolutely," Kayla replied. "You can take the lead on finding us the right candidate."

"Great." Courtney smiled. "So what else?" She needed more.

Kayla continued. "Well, Ethan and I have looked at our marketing and communications department, and since we've merged Graham International's cosmetic division with Adams Cosmetics, there's definitely room for improvement."

"I agree."

"I would like nothing better than to give you the director of marketing slot, but as you know, that's already filled." Kayla noticed the frown creasing Courtney's forehead and said, "But we would like to offer you the associate director of marketing and communications slot."

A smile formed on Courtney's mouth.

"Bryan will continue to lead the department, creating our annual plan, collaborating with our sales force, handling the budget and management of the team, but under his tutelage your focus will be on the creative side of event planning, public relations and advertising campaigns for new products. How does that sound?"

"It sounds great."

"You don't mind working as a team with Bryan?"

"No, we've been doing that already."

Kayla smiled. "So I've heard. He's told us about the great ideas you've come up with previously, so we think this is a good fit for you."

"So do I," Courtney said. "This is just the kind of thing I've wanted to sink my teeth into, so I happily accept. When do I start?"

"How does now sound?" Kayla said. "It'll be a little crazy until we find your replacement, but do you think you can handle both jobs given your new love life?"

Courtney chuckled to herself. She was wondering when the conversation was going to get around to Jasper. Try as she might, sometimes the line of business and family blurred for Kayla. "I'll be just fine. Jasper knows I want a larger role at the company."

"So you've spoken to him about our business?" Kayla asked testily.

Courtney immediately noticed the aggressive tone in Kayla's voice and returned it in kind. "We've discussed how I've been viewed as a child for years," she responded curtly, "who should be happy with a pat on the head from the public. And that it's time I take my rightful place in this company."

Kayla sighed. "I'm sorry if you took offense to my question."

"How could I not, Kayla?" Courtney said, her eyes narrowing. "You were insinuating that I'd told him company secrets or something, which couldn't be further from the truth. Jasper and I don't have the time or inclination to talk about business in bed when there are much more fun things to do."

Kayla blushed and chuckled, which immediately helped ease the tension in the room. "Oh my God, Courtney. That's what I love about you. You just say whatever is on your mind, no matter the consequences. I envy that."

"I know sometimes that can get me into trouble," Courtney said. "But in this instance, I have to say I'm disappointed in you, Kay. You were quick to leap to the conclusion that Jasper is out to harm our family. We all thought the same thing about Ethan. Or is that what this is all about? Is turnabout fair play?"

Kayla paused as if she was considering that scenario. "I really hadn't thought about that. I just get riled up whenever Andrew Jackson's name is mentioned, and to know Jasper is related to him, I admit it does not sit well with me. I'm concerned about you. I don't want you to get hurt."

"Well don't be," Courtney said affirmatively. "I've got this. And even if I didn't, it's my mistake to make. You guys have to let me fall flat on my face."

"You're my baby sister, Courtney," Kayla said. "That's hard for me to do."

"Try harder," Courtney said, rising from her chair. "Because Jasper isn't going away. I hope you're prepared because Mother invited him to our family dinner on Saturday night."

"Oh, Lord!" Kayla rolled her eyes.

"Buckle up," Courtney said, "'cause it might be a bumpy night."

* * *

"So you're thinking about permanently staying in the U.S.?" Mark asked Jasper once he'd returned to Punta Cana.

"I'm giving it great thought," Jasper said. "There is no way Courtney is going to leave her family, whereas I can be stationed anywhere. We have the two hotels here in the Dominican Republic plus a hotel in Florida. And my mother is in Marietta. I would love to be closer to her, especially after her accident. She looks more fragile to me now."

"I understand being closer to your mother, but you hate the U.S.," Mark said. "Or so you've told me. You've always said how much you like being close to the ocean and a walk away from the beach. Are you really ready to give that all up for a woman?"

"Quite possibly," Jasper said. He saw the surprised look on Mark's face. "Don't look so stunned. It's hard for me to believe it too. One day, I'm happy in this solitary life, but the next day I meet Courtney and I realize I don't want to be alone. I was so busy running away from the ghosts of the past that I wasn't letting anyone in."

"And you've let Courtney in?"

"Way in." Jasper smiled broadly. "She knows the truth."

"That you're Andrew Jackson's son?" Mark said.

Jasper nodded. "And despite knowing all that, she still wants to be with me."

"Sounds like she's a pretty amazing woman."

"She is," Jasper said. "And I can't wait to get back to her."

Chapter 13

Jasper sighed wearily as the taxi drove him to the restaurant to meet Courtney's family. Courtney had felt it would be less intimidating if he met her family in a public place versus their family estate. This would ensure that they were on their best behavior. He'd just gotten in from Punta Cana two hours before after a long workweek. He'd had just enough time to get back to the hotel, have a quick shower and get back on the road.

He'd called ahead and told Courtney he would meet her there and she was waiting for him outside Chops Lobster Bar. He was thankful because he didn't relish going in to face her family without her by his side. Not that he was afraid or anything, but he respected Courtney and wanted to avoid causing a scene. Yet Jasper suspected that his presence would cause one despite his best efforts.

Courtney looked amazing. She was wearing a navy one-shoulder dress with beading along the side that stopped above her knee. The silhouette was fitted and cleverly showed her figure without being too revealing.

A smile lit up Courtney's face as he approached. Jasper looked dapper in a sleek charcoal designer suit. His hair and goatee had been freshly trimmed and he smelled woodsy, like cedar and sandalwood with a splash of citrus and lavender. It was divine. She couldn't wait for the night to be over so she could ravish him. "You made it!" She let out a sigh of relief and wrapped her arms around his neck. "I was beginning to worry."

Jasper grasped one of her hands and squeezed. "I wouldn't let you down. I know what a big deal this is for you, meeting your family and all."

"I'm just happy you're here." Courtney pressed her lips hotly against his. She'd missed him. He'd only been gone a week, but it had felt like an eternity.

The Adamses had secured a private dining room, and when Courtney and Jasper entered, everyone turned their heads. Jasper noticed several couples and an older couple mingling in the room as they sipped cocktails.

"Everything will be fine," Jasper whispered in Courtney's ear as they approached the group.

"From your lips to God's ears."

Gabrielle was the first to approach them. "Jasper," she said, her arms wide open, "so happy you could make it tonight."

Jasper accepted the gracious greeting and allowed himself to be enveloped in the brunette's arms for a hug. He could see why Shane was taken with her. She was a natural beauty with warm brown skin, almond-shaped eyes and round cheeks. "Thank you," Jasper said when they'd let go. "I'm happy to meet you."

"Courtney has said great things about you," Gabrielle said, "so we couldn't wait to meet you."

I just bet, Jasper thought. He doubted the Adams family wanted to meet him in the slightest. It was probably tantamount to sacrilege that a Jackson was even in their midst.

Courtney winked at Gabby for breaking the ice. "Come, you have to meet the rest of the family." She walked over to Shane first on the far side of the group. "This is my brother, Shane."

Shane firmly shook Jasper's hand, but Jasper could tell he was sizing him up. "Nice to meet you," Jasper said.

"Likewise," Shane replied.

They moved from one end of the group to the other. She was leaving her parents for last, which would hopefully give her mother enough time to get her father under control. "And this is my older sister, Kayla, and her husband, Ethan Graham, and my adorable nephew, Alexander."

Courtney took the infant right out of Kayla's arms. She nuzzled the boy with her nose. "Isn't my nephew the cutest thing in the world?" She moved closer to Jasper so he could see him.

"We think so," Kayla responded first. "Pleasure to meet you, Jasper." She eyed him suspiciously.

"You as well." He inclined his head as he looked down at her son. "He's a fine-looking boy."

"Thank you," Ethan said, and offered his hand. "Ethan."

"Jasper." Jasper noticed that Ethan didn't immediately let go of his hand.

Instead Ethan leaned forward and pulled him slightly away from the group. "It won't be easy becoming a part of this clan," he said. "They don't cotton well to outsiders. You'll have to prove yourself."

"I'm up for the challenge," Jasper whispered back.

"What do you think they're talking about?" Courtney asked Kayla as she returned her nephew to his mother.

"Ethan's probably warning him to run in the other direction," Kayla said, laughing.

Courtney chuckled. "You're probably right." She strode toward the men in private conversation. "If I can break this up, I'd like to introduce you to my parents."

Jasper inclined his head to Ethan, silently thanking him for the warning before grasping hold of Courtney's hand and walking toward her parents.

Byron Adams might have been Jasper's height, but he was still every bit as intimidating as Courtney had said he would be. Despite the occasion and his well-tailored suit, Byron had a scowl on his mahogany face. Jasper doubted very much that he'd wanted this introduction, but it was inevitable.

"Daddy," Courtney said gingerly, smiling at her mother the entire time, "I'd like you to meet Jasper Jackson, my boyfriend." She'd added the last words at the last second and she could feel her father cringe outwardly, but he said nothing.

"Mr. Adams." Jasper held out his hand first as a gesture of goodwill. "Pleasure to meet you, sir."

Byron stared down at his hand for several long moments and Jasper thought he wasn't going to shake it, but then Byron glanced at his wife to his side and extended his hand. "No need to call me sir."

Jasper nodded. "Mrs. Adams, I presume." He came to Courtney's mother. He wasn't surprised by her startling beauty. Even though she had to be in her fifties, Jasper saw Courtney in her. She had the same smooth café-au-lait skin that Courtney and Shane had and the same piercing green eyes.

"Yes." Elizabeth smiled warmly at him. "I'm so happy to meet you, Jasper." She leaned over and kissed his cheek. "Courtney has spoken highly of you."

"Thank you." He made sure not to call her ma'am so as not to offend Mr. Adams. "You're every bit as lovely as your daughter."

Elizabeth Adams beamed with pride.

"Well, she gets it honest," Byron huffed at her side.

Elizabeth turned to glare at her husband. "How about an aperitif?"

Half an hour later, the Adams family sat down to share a meal at a large twelve-person table. Courtney's parents, Shane and Gabrielle, Kayla and Ethan were at one end of the table while Kayla's best friend, Piper, and Ethan's right-hand man, Daniel Walker, sat in the middle along with Courtney and Jasper. Courtney had suggested inviting them so that Piper and Daniel could help keep the evening light.

The only person missing was Tea. She arrived shortly after they were all seated.

"Tea, honey." Courtney rushed over to give her best friend a hug. "Glad you're here." She needed positive reinforcements tonight, and she wanted to ensure a friendly environment for Jasper.

"Sorry, I'm late," Tea said, removing her coat, which a server immediately ushered away. "How's it going?"

"No one's shot anyone, so I'd say we're okay. Are you hungry?" Courtney asked, tucking her arm in Tea's arm. "Mother selected a great four-course meal."

"Sounds good. I'm ravenous."

Jasper smiled as the two women walked toward the table.

"Has the family roasted you yet?" Tea asked, looking Jasper up and down. This was her first look at the man who'd sprung her best friend. She'd never seen Courtney this giddy, this *happy*. And she could see why. He was definitely what the doctor ordered: tall, somewhere around six feet, with skin as dark as midnight and handsome, chiseled features and a strong jaw. Courtney had done good.

Jasper knew the woman had to be Tea. Courtney had described her as Latin, feisty and straight talking and he liked her instantly. "Actually, things are going quite well." He smiled smoothly, showing her a perfect set of white teeth. "I thought I'd be charcoal dust by now, but I've managed to keep an even color."

Tea laughed. "I like you, Jasper," she said. "You've got a sense of humor. And that'll serve you well with this group." She glanced behind him to see Courtney's family staring at them.

Tea took a seat and Jasper joined them at the table and pulled out a chair for Courtney. He liked that she had a close-knit family and great friends. He envied her. Other than his mother, he wasn't close to many. Sure, he'd had his grandfather who'd passed away when he was twenty, and he'd learned the construction business from his uncle Duke, but they hadn't talked much the past few years. Right then, Jasper resolved to make a better effort of keeping in touch with his uncle. He might not have a father, but there was no reason he couldn't have a father figure.

The rest of the evening didn't go nearly as bad as Jasper had envisioned. Other than Kayla and Byron grilling him about his background, education and hotel business, everyone else seemed to be taking their relationship in stride. That was until his father strode into their private dining room. He was with Monica and another woman who Jasper assumed to be his new wife, Blythe.

Jasper turned to Courtney and he saw her face turn as white as a ghost. This was exactly what she had feared. Drama.

Shane instantly jumped out of his chair and put a hand out to stop Andrew from coming any farther into the room before Jasper could even get out of his seat. "You have no place here, Andrew."

"Oh, am I interrupting something?" Andrew asked innocently with a thick Southern drawl. He peered over Shane to survey the room and its occupants. His dark eyes glanced over to Byron, who had Elizabeth's hand on his arm, probably in an effort to keep him from making a scene.

"You know damn well you are," Jasper said, coming to Shane's aid. "Leave."

"Well, if it isn't my son." Andrew chuckled, but there was no denying the disgust on his face as he surveyed Jasper. "Eating with the enemy."

"I thought I made it clear to you last week that I want *no association* with you." Jasper said the words loud enough so the entire room could hear, especially Courtney's father. He needed him to know that he had nothing to do with Andrew crashing their dinner.

"And your *message* was received, loud and clear." Andrew gave him a steely stare. "I just happened to be at Chops for an evening out with my beautiful wife *and daughter*." He emphasized the word for Jasper's effect. "And we were looking for our seat."

"I just bet you were," Jasper said.

Seconds later, the restaurant manager was at the doorway. "Mr. and Mrs. Jackson, I believe you are in the wrong area," he said. "This is a private event. Please allow me to take you to your seats."

Andrew glared at everyone in the room before whispering to Jasper, "I warned you." He rasped, "You had better be on your guard."

Jasper shuddered.

Andrew tucked his arm in his wife's. "Let's go, my darlings. There's nothing here of importance."

Monica gave Jasper a triumphant smile on her way out.

The room erupted with chatter. "Can you believe the nerve?" "That man has no shame!" Jasper could barely hear any of them, because he felt as if all eyes were on him. The chilling warning Andrew had just given him was impossible to ignore.

Slowly, Jasper made his way back to the table, but he could feel Byron Adams's eyes boring a hole in his head. When he got to the table, Courtney wasn't there.

"Where's Courtney?" Jasper asked Tea, looking around.

"Dunno," Tea said. "After your father left she ran out of the room."

Jasper sucked in a breath. That's what he was afraid of. That she would be so upset by his father that she would create a rift between them right when they were just figuring things out.

"Wait!" Courtney yelled to Andrew's back as he, Blythe and Monica made their way down the hall.

Surprised, Andrew spun around on his cowboy boots. "And what can I do for you, princess?"

Courtney hated that he used the nickname Jasper had given her. "What you can do for me," Courtney said, "is to leave Jasper and my family alone."

"How dare you talk to my father like that! You've known Jasper for what, like two seconds?" Monica snapped her fingers.

"Darlin', darlin'." Andrew grasped Monica's elbow. "Why don't you and your mother go and get seated? I'll be right in."

Monica gave Courtney the evil eye before guiding her mother away.

"Listen, little lady." Andrew's voice turned deadly cold. "Don't you go telling me about *my son!*"

"Your son wants nothing to do with you," Courtney responded with equal fervor. "Stop inserting yourself in his life."

"And why is that?" Andrew asked. "Because of you and your damn family! You've turned my son against me."

Courtney was taken aback by Andrew's anger toward her. "Jasper hasn't been a part of your life for many years, Mr. Jackson. This shouldn't come as a surprise to you. I had nothing to do with his decision."

"I don't believe that for one second," Andrew hissed. "Your entire family has had it out for me since day one, and I know you're telling my son I'm the devil incarnate."

"You're delusional." Courtney turned to move away, but Andrew jerked her arm back until she was inches away from him.

"I'm not finished with you." He leaned down and glared at her.

"Well, I'm done with you," Courtney responded. "Keep coming, keep trying your best to hurt my family, Mr. Jackson. Because you will find we're a close-knit group and nothing can break us."

"You think you're pretty fearless, huh?" Andrew stared at her menacingly. "Well, you're wrong, *princess*. You and your family have taken enough away from me. I will make you pay for turning my son against me. I will make you pay dearly."

Courtney swallowed hard as a cold chill went right through her. For some reason, she believed Andrew capable of getting back at her, but would he really harm her physically? Or would he come after her family as he'd always done?

She quickly snatched her arm away and rushed back to the private dining room. When she returned, Jasper rushed to greet her. "Babe, where were you?" he asked.

"Having a word with your father."

"Do you really think that was wise?" Jasper asked.

"I can take care of myself. He was all smoke and no fire." Courtney laughed nervously. She decided against telling Jasper what his father had said. If he knew his father had just threatened her, the chasm that was already between father and son would only widen. She could handle whatever Andrew Jackson threw at her. She was an Adams, after all.

Chapter 14

"That was some dinner last night," Kayla said when Courtney met her at the country club for a game of tennis. Kayla was ready for battle in her royal-blue tennis skirt and matching shirt.

Kayla had offered to come to the estate where the family had a perfectly good tennis court, but Courtney had opted for a less hostile environment. Ever since the introductory dinner to meet Jasper, her father had been staring daggers at Courtney from across the dining-room table. She knew he wanted to say something about Andrew being Jasper's father and causing a ruckus, but surprisingly he was holding his tongue. Her mother was no doubt behind his restraint.

"Yeah, it was," Courtney finally said, throwing down her tennis bag and removing her jacket. It was a slightly cool morning and she needed something on her arms to cover her sleeveless fuchsia tennis dress. Her honey-blond hair was slicked back away from her face and she wore no makeup.

Courtney removed her racket from her bag. "Are you ready to get beat?" she asked.

"How many sets are we playing?" Kayla asked, pulling a coin out of her purse.

"Best of three?"

"Sounds good to me," Kayla said, tossing the coin in the air. "Call it."

"Tails."

The coin landed on heads on the pavement. "I serve," Kayla said, smiling.

Courtney knew her sister was going to use it to her advantage to take the point, but she was prepared for it. Kayla served the ball exactly as Courtney knew she would, but Courtney's racket connected with the ball and sent it right back at her. They continued volleying. It was only when Kayla ran a near-miss ball and used her famous backhand stroke that Courtney lost the point.

"Fifteen—love," Kayla said, smiling smugly across the net.

Courtney won the next point. "Fifteen—all," she announced.

They continued their game in much the same way as they always had. The score rallied back and forth between the two of them, 1–1 with each of them winning a set. When they were on their last set, Courtney was in the lead 2–3.

"Break point!" Courtney yelled when Kayla tossed the ball in the air. She hit the ball forcefully and it whizzed right by Courtney's nose. "What the hell was that?" she yelled, throwing down her racquet and rushing toward the net.

"What are you talking about?" Kayla asked, coming forward.

"You damn near hit my face." Courtney was furious. "This—" she pointed to her face "—is still a commodity to this family, at least for another few weeks."

"Oh, Courtney, stop being so dramatic," Kayla said. "I didn't intend to hit you."

"What's your beef, Kayla?"

"I don't have any beef."

"No? Are you sure you're not upset about dinner last night?" Courtney asked.

"Of course not," Kayla replied. "Jasper was quite charming. He can't help where he comes from."

"So you finally realize that?"

"I do," Kayla said. "But that doesn't mean that the two of you are the right fit. I mean really, Courtney, he lives in the Dominican Republic and you live here. How is a relationship between you two going to work? Or had you not thought about that among all your romantic notions?"

Tears welled up in Courtney's eyes. She knew Kayla had a point, but she didn't have to be so brutal. "Gosh, Kay, do you have to sound so harsh?"

The moment she saw the tears in Courtney's eyes, Kayla felt horrible. She never wanted to make her baby sister cry. She was supposed to be protecting her. "I'm so sorry, Courtney. That was horribly insensitive of me. I know you have strong feelings for Jasper, but even you must see the hurdles you're facing. Both families are against you and you're in a long-distance relationship. Is it really worth all this heartache?"

In that moment, knowing that she could lose Jasper, Courtney realized she was in love with him.

* * *

"Hey, what's wrong?" Jasper asked when they were lying in the king-size bed at his hotel suite the following evening. After a long day at the office, Jasper had had a picnic delivered, complete with champagne, fruits, sliced meats, pâté, cheeses and French baguettes. He'd wanted to make it up to her since he'd had to deal with some business on Sunday and hadn't had a chance to see if there was any fallout from dinner.

Courtney sipped on the bubbly, but had hardly touched the food. Jasper searched her eyes for a sign of what could be bothering her, but they were unreadable.

"My sister made me think about a problem in our relationship," she finally said after several moments had passed.

Why was he not surprised? Although Kayla Graham had been more than pleasant to him at the dinner, he got the distinct impression that she did not want him with Courtney. "What did she say?"

"She reminded me of our living arrangements," Courtney said, sitting upright on the bed. "That I live here and you live in DR. Even though subconsciously I knew it, we've never really talked about this. I mean, how do we make this—" she pointed to the two of them "—work?"

"Well." Jasper rubbed his goatee thoughtfully. "I've been thinking about that."

"And?" Courtney's voice rose slightly. "You know I can't leave my family or Adams Cosmetics, and I just got my dream job and my rightful place there."

"I realize that, Courtney."

"Well, then?"

"I will move back here," Jasper replied, looking her square in the face with no hesitation. "You know, make Atlanta my home base."

"You would do that?"

Jasper nodded. "It's why I went back to Punta Cana to talk it over with my head of development, Mark. I don't need to be on-site to oversee the building of the new hotel now that I have a contractor I can trust. I moved an ocean away to put distance between me and my father, and apparently even an ocean wasn't enough. The man has haunted me and probably always will."

"Are you sure about this?" Courtney asked. She didn't want him to regret his decision and later come to resent her for taking him away from a life he loved. "You love the beach and the ocean. You love the carefree lifestyle on the island."

"I do," Jasper admitted. "But you and me—" he pointed to her and again to him as she had done "—is more important. How can we build the framework for a relationship if an ocean is separating us?"

"It would be pretty difficult."

"Well, then it's settled," Jasper said. "And since I will be staying here, I think it's time you met my mother."

Courtney gulped hard. "Your mother?"

Jasper noticed the concern that came across Courtney's face. "Don't worry, she'll love you."

"Don't you think it's a little too soon?"

"Soon?" Jasper asked. "I've already met your parents, heck, your entire family."

"And look how well that turned out," she said.

"My mother is one of the kindest, gentlest people you're ever going to meet," Jasper said. "She will adore you from the minute she meets you, just like I did."

Courtney smiled broadly. "Hmm…I don't recall it being instantaneous. If I remember correctly, you were going to leave me, the princess, on the side of the road."

Jasper pulled Courtney into his arms. "True, but I came back for you," he said as he brushed his lips across hers.

The sweet intensity sent Courtney swirling, and all she could mutter was "And I'm oh so glad you did" before wrapping her arms around Jasper's neck and lowering herself to the bed. Jasper's full body weight came on top of her and Courtney welcomed the feeling. Their tongues mated and danced in a delicious game of cat and mouse.

He moved from her lips to her earlobe and then to her neck. He kissed, licked and teased, sending flames shooting through Courtney. His hot tongue left a trail as wide as Texas and she responded in turn, brimming with passion. He stopped to sample her breasts, and it was there that he took an inordinate amount of time. He pushed down the tank top she was wearing to wet them with his tongue, and they became taut with tension. He eased the tension with delicious flicks and licks across her nipples.

As he took liberties with her breasts, she allowed her hands to roam Jasper. She was eager to explore the angles of his muscular body. When she found the hard velvet part of him in his jeans, she squeezed purposefully and he pulsed underneath her hand. Jasper let out a groan.

"I think we're both wearing too many clothes, don'tcha think?" he murmured. Every touch, every taste of Courtney was firing a need deep inside him that needed to be quenched.

Instantly, they were tearing at each other's clothes, eager to be naked. When they were both clothes free, they reached for each other and tumbled back onto the bed.

Jasper took charge. His hands roamed downward so they could play and dally with her nether lips. When he confirmed she was wet and ready for him, he sheathed himself so he could root himself deep inside her.

"Please, I need you inside me...." Courtney made whimpering noises, begging him to take her.

"With pleasure," he said, burying himself deep within her sweet haven.

She raised her hips as he thrust in and out, and the bed squeaked underneath them. Their cries and groans echoed throughout the room. Before his release could claim him, Jasper switched positions until Courtney was kneeling and facing the headboard, and he took her from behind. He quickened the rhythm and Courtney thought she might die from pleasure. The position was extremely stimulating because it gave Jasper easy access to stroke her breasts and play with her womanly lips, but also because it hit her sweet spot. The force of his thrust had her coming and flying over the edge. Jasper came right behind her, yelling out his joy, and Courtney fell forward on the bed.

As the night darkened, Courtney lost track of time because they were voracious for each other. They made love on a chair, on the floor with Jasper thrusting into her and her gripping him as wave after wave of sheer delight coursed through her. They made love again on the credenza in the suite, in the shower and then finally in front of the cheval mirror.

"In front of the mirror?" Courtney raised an eyebrow when Jasper set her on the floor.

"Yes, I want to see your face when I make you come," Jasper croaked hungrily as he dropped from the bed to one knee.

Jasper shamelessly spread her legs and Courtney gasped when she saw his mouth on her derriere, licking her naked cheeks. But it also felt good—so she didn't protest. She didn't stop him when his tongue found its way to her aching clitoris and he teased it and then bathed it with broad strokes. "Jasper—" she shouted, swaying until she found

Jasper's strong hands there to steady her as her orgasm hit her full force.

"Was it good?" Jasper asked as he rose to his feet behind her.

Courtney blushed. "You know it was."

"I'm not done yet," Jasper said.

He lowered himself on the bed and then placed Courtney above him so she could ride him. He positioned her in front of the mirror and from that vantage point she could see the moment his erection reached her brown curls. The mirror revealed the sight of him pushing and disappearing inside her. It also showed a wanton woman with disheveled hair, swollen lips and heavy-lidded eyes. Courtney reveled in her sexuality and bounced on Jasper, her bottom jiggling.

Jasper was enjoying watching Courtney get off. "Yes, baby, you are in control, ride me!"

With her legs on either side of his muscular thighs, Courtney slammed into him and Jasper arched his hips upward so he could pound into her. Courtney panted and threw her head back. Her breasts jutted forward and Jasper used it as an opportunity to ravish them—suckling and pulling one and then the other into his mouth. Courtney surrendered and gripped Jasper's shoulders, screaming out his name as her orgasm overtook her.

"I'm going to come," Jasper said as pleasure roared through him. He pushed hard one final time before he collapsed back to the bed.

When they were done, neither of them could move; all they could do was give each other a satisfied smile before drifting off to sleep.

Andrew Jackson fumed as he sat in the study of his twenty-bedroom plantation on the outskirts of Marietta later that night. He sat at a large mahogany desk with the lamp on low lighting. A half-full cognac decanter sat next to his empty glass. Andrew reached for it again and poured himself another generous glass. He was still smarting over the fact that his son had deserted him publicly in front of all those damn Adamses a week ago. Andrew could spit he was so angry.

He'd given that boy everything money had to offer. He had the best toys, the finest clothes and a superb education, bar none. He'd even bought an Aston Martin in preparation for his sixteenth birthday, but Jasper had just spit it back in his face. Told him he was going to live with his mama. He was just as ungrateful as she was.

The only reason he'd married Abigail was that he'd knocked her up. He'd been drunk the night he met her and on a bender. He'd just found out that his former best friend was going to marry Elizabeth. The knowledge tore through his heart like a bullet. He still had the scars because he'd never recovered from the wound.

Nevertheless, the moment he'd found out he was going to be a father, he'd slapped a ring on the backwoods girl and married her. His father would have expected nothing less from a true Southern gentleman. Not to mention the fact that she might be carrying his heir. And she had been. She'd tried to have other children, but Abigail and pregnancy didn't mix after that, and she'd suffered two miscarriages in the span of three years.

If she wasn't going to be a broodmare, Andrew hadn't seen much use for her. It wasn't long before he began straying from the marital bed. Of course, he had been having affairs before then, because despite fixing her up in the best clothes, hair and makeup, Abigail was just a poor country girl with no skills in the bedroom. She eventually got the hint that he had no feelings for her whatsoever and took a hike.

The one good thing she'd done was produce a son. His son. Jasper had been the joy of his life from the day he was born, which was why he'd fought tooth and nail to keep him. It was only when Jasper had found out some of his business secrets that he'd had to let him go. And he had done so, because deep down he always thought Jasper would see the error of his ways and come back someday. Kind of the way he thought Elizabeth might leave Byron and come back to him, but neither of those scenarios had ever happened.

Instead he'd married or *settled* again. This time to his current wife, Blythe, who already had a daughter, Monica. Blythe had been a single mother working as an administrative assistant at Jax Cosmetics. She'd been happy to get out of her nowhere job and move up to the house on the hill with her daughter. She was tall and a beauty, a real nice arm piece, but he didn't love her either. He doubted he would ever love a woman other than Elizabeth. And Monica, well, she was truly the son he never had. She was cunning and ruthless, a real ballbuster. She was just like him, but she *still* wasn't Jasper.

The more time passed, the angrier Andrew got. Over the years, he'd had some slightly successful attempts at damaging Byron's company by stealing a couple of employees, ensuring that their shipments broke down and things like that. But none of them were as brilliant as convincing the vengeful actress Noelle Warner to come to his aid, thanks to Ethan's enormously large ego in thinking he could have an ex working for him with no repercussions.

Unfortunately Noelle had been caught, but even though Ethan had threatened her, Noelle had been smart enough not to give him up. She knew the consequences of betraying Andrew Jackson.

Andrew had even convinced that lush of an account executive, James Burton, to steal from his own daughter, Gabrielle, and leak AC's prototype to the press. He'd tried for the lady herself, but that darn Gabrielle had a lot of spunk and told him to take a flying leap. Not many people impressed him, but she had because even with her head over a barrel, she would not give in to his blackmail. He wished she had, because she was a darn good chemist whom he would have liked working for him.

And still, none of his shenanigans stopped those Adamses. Ecstasy was still beating Jax Cosmetics' Noelle in the latest sales reports he'd received, even though it was a cheaper imitation. And rumor had it that they had another fragrance on the horizon.

Andrew suspected they all thought they were smarter and better than him. He was born into a wealthy aristocrat lineage, and his great-great-grandfather had owned slaves. But Byron? He came from nothing, from the Atlanta slums. He'd had to work with Carter Graham for years before starting his own company. And his measly eleven-room mansion was nothing in comparison to the twenty-bedroom plantation Andrew had inherited, along with a hundred acres of prime land.

What did Elizabeth see in Byron anyway to marry him, have three children and start a company with him? What would it take to stop them? Andrew was going to have to take desperate measures to finally put a hole in Byron's sails once and for all. He would not let Jasper become a part of their family. He would stop it at all costs.

The door to his study opened. Andrew saw the visitor and motioned him forward. He slid a large envelope of cash across the mahogany desk. "Make it look like an accident."

Chapter 15

"What are you so nervous about?" Tea asked Courtney when she dropped by the Adams estate to help Courtney pick out an appropriate ensemble to meet Jasper's mother in. Tea was sitting on Courtney's king-size bed in her master suite.

Courtney's bedroom was much like the lady herself, over-the-top and done in white, ivory and biscuit. She had an oversize four-poster canopy bed with white bedding and large pillows of various sizes, a huge cheval mirror, regal Italian statues and a crystal chandelier with ornate ceiling moldings.

"It's too soon." Courtney held up a black sheath dress and Tea shook her head.

"Boring and it's not you. You're not going to the office. You're going to meet his mama."

Courtney sighed. She'd already tried on half a dozen outfits and eighty-sixed them all.

"He's already met your entire family," Tea continued. "It only seems fair that you should meet his."

"I know," Courtney said, "it's just that given *who* he is, he had to meet my family to allay their fears that he wasn't Andrew's lackey spying on us, but this…this…"

"This what?" Tea asked. "This means you two are getting serious? Well, he *is* relocating his home office to Atlanta and rearranging his life just to be close to you."

"When you put it like that, it makes me seem hypocritical and unyielding."

Tea shrugged. "If the shoe fits."

"You know me." Courtney touched her chest. "I've never done long term. I was worse than Shane when it came to relationships. At the first sign of a guy getting attached, I would run for the hills. At least Shane kept his women around a few months."

"And you're afraid of what this means?"

"I mean this is serious, meeting his mother," Courtney said, wringing her hands and pacing the floor.

"And you're wondering what's next?"

Courtney nodded.

"Have you discussed long term?" Tea asked. "You know, what your expectations are?"

"No, I mean we've had a couple of other hurdles to deal with."

"Then don't leap to conclusions," Tea said logically. "Be yourself and I'm sure Jasper's mother will love you."

"I hope so."

"I don't know about this," Courtney said on the drive from Atlanta to the outskirts of Marietta. Jasper was driving her to meet his mother, and Courtney was extremely nervous. The more she'd thought about it, the more anxious she'd become. She'd grown up in a life of privilege and glamour, whereas Jasper's mother had come from very humble beginnings.

It's why she'd settled on a simple outfit of skinny jeans with a white peasant shirt and a chunky belt. She didn't want Jasper's mother to think she was a pampered princess.

With one hand still on the wheel of the Maserati he'd recently purchased, Jasper reached across to squeeze Courtney's hand. "You'll be fine. Mom's going to love you."

"I hope so," Courtney said, fidgeting in her chair. She'd watched the scenery change from metropolitan Atlanta to the rural countryside of Marietta during their ride.

"You know, I wasn't this nervous when I met your folks, and trust me, I had a lot more to be worried about given my association to Andrew."

"Well, mothers are notoriously harder on their sons' girlfriends," Courtney responded tartly. "It's a fact."

Jasper laughed. "Is that so? Well, then we just have to break open that bottle of chardonnay you brought." He inclined his head to the wine box on the floor of the Maserati. "Sooner rather than later to loosen you up."

"No!" Courtney shook her head. "Then your mother will think I'm a lush."

"Courtney, baby," Jasper crooned, "you're going to have to loosen up. My mother doesn't bite."

The car turned off the main road onto a dirty road with a sign that read Cartwright Farm. As they drove, Courtney could see the farm was set on many acres of land. Courtney saw horses and cows grazing in a pasture surrounded by large white fences. She saw a barn and stables just before the car stopped in front of the main house, where she assumed his mother lived. It was a two-story rectangular-shaped farmhouse with a wraparound front porch with white railings.

A petite woman with big dark curls that reached her shoulders came flying out the front door in jeans and a plaid shirt. "You're here."

Jasper was first out of the car. He was coming around to open Courtney's door when his mother came bounding down the steps. A little too quickly for his liking, since she'd just been given clearance to walk and was still in physical therapy.

"Mama, be careful," he said, rushing to her side at the porch steps. "You know Doc said to watch that hip."

"I know, I know." She slapped his hand away. "I just can't wait to meet Courtney." She stood outside the car expectantly.

Jasper walked over and opened Courtney's door. "Mama, I'd like you to meet Courtney Adams. Courtney, this is my mother, Abigail Jackson."

"It's so great to meet you." Abigail rushed forward and pulled Courtney into a warm hug. "I've heard a lot about you." She pulled away so she could assess Courtney further. "And you're every bit as beautiful as Jasper said you were."

"Thank you, Mrs. Jackson." Courtney smiled and knew instantly that she had nothing to fear. Jasper's mother was a woman to love. She had an oval face, big brown eyes and a wide smile.

"Please call me Abigail," she said, circling her arm through Courtney's and walking her toward the house. "We have lots to talk about."

Hours later, Courtney realized that Abigail Jackson was every bit as genuine as Jasper had said, more so in her opinion. She'd learned that Jasper had been a handful as a child, always climbing trees, trying to play with alligators in the pond and generally pushing the limits. If a chocolate brother could blush, Jasper did when Abigail pulled out several photo albums and showed pictures of Jasper with bad haircuts in high school.

"It was the style back then," Jasper said.

After they'd shared a lovely brunch of quiche, summer salad and sweet tea, Jasper extended a tour of the farm and the ranch by horseback.

Courtney turned to Abigail for approval.

"I don't mind one bit," Abigail said. "There's nothing better than being outdoors on the farm with the fresh air in your face and filling your lungs."

"Then you're on," Courtney said, smiling at Jasper.

After they'd saddled up, Jasper on a black Clydesdale horse and Courtney on a beautiful palomino with a gold coat and white tail, they were off to explore the farm. Jasper pointed out the barn that housed the cows, the chicken coop and the pigpen. Then he galloped off into the distance. Courtney had to give her mare a little kick just to keep up with him. She found him dismounted and the horse grazing by a nearby pond.

"Hey, you." She was out of breath when she climbed off the mare. "You left me in your dust."

He turned and pulled Courtney into his arms. "Because I knew you'd keep up." He smiled and bent down to brush his full lips across hers. When he lifted his head, he said, "I've wanted to do that all day." He smacked her on the bottom.

"Have you, you bad boy?" she snickered.

"Indeed," Jasper said, and then turned back to face the pond. "Don't you just love it out here, the peace, the quiet, the serenity?"

"I do," Courtney said, watching him underneath hooded lashes. She'd seen another side of Jasper today—the side that was a son, caretaker, friend. And she'd loved it, loved him. In her wildest dreams, she would never have imagined that an island fling could have turned into so much more, that she would find her soul mate. But she did. Jasper was her soul mate. "I'm going to enjoy visiting the farm."

Jasper spun around to look at her. "So you'd come again?"

"Absolutely," she stated.

"You look stunning," Jasper said the following weekend when Courtney emerged from the master bathroom of his new penthouse apartment in Ansley Park. She was wearing a strapless yellow sequined dress that was skin-tight and hugged her delicious curves from the swell of her breasts to her hips. It was a daring color that not many women could have pulled off, but Courtney wore it well.

"You look pretty good too," Courtney said as she came forward and straightened out the blue handkerchief in his tuxedo pocket. Jasper was wearing the heck out of his black tuxedo sans tie. "Are you ready to go spend some money on some jewelry to benefit the Partnership for Domestic Violence?"

"I must confess that getting dressed up for charity events isn't really my thing," Jasper replied. "I'd much prefer to be in jeans and a T-shirt. But I believe in the cause, so yes, I will open my wallet, perhaps for something for you?"

Courtney liked that idea. "Well, there won't be many more of these events that I *have* to attend," she replied. "I am interviewing candidates to take over my spot as Adams Cosmetics spokeswoman."

Jasper tugged her closer to him and peered into her eyes. "Are you sure you're ready to give up the limelight?" He'd watched her on that photo shoot in Punta Cana and saw how at ease she was in front of a camera. Was she ready to take a backseat and not be the center of attention?

Courtney smiled, showing her pretty white teeth. "I am. It's time for a changing of the guard. And I'm ready to prove that I'm just as talented as my siblings."

"And you're already doing it," Jasper said. Courtney had jumped headfirst into her new role as associate director and was working closely with Bryan on Bliss's new campaign.

Courtney and Jasper arrived at the Four Seasons Hotel in downtown Atlanta a short while later. After he left his Maserati with the valet, they walked the red carpet to the front door. Several local photographers and a camera crew were already on the sidewalk taking photos.

Jasper released Courtney's arm so she could take photos, and he stood along the sidelines admiring her as she posed in front of the cameras.

"Ms. Adams, you're looking lovely as always," one of the cameramen said, smiling.

"Thank you." Courtney gave him a wink. "And I'm wearing Adams Cosmetics' latest scent, Ecstasy." She always mentioned AC products whenever possible.

Courtney left the red carpet and Jasper joined her arm with his. "You know you had the guy salivating," Jasper whispered in her ear.

"Oh, he's a teddy bear," she murmured as they walked in.

The hostess, Anne Burke, was standing in the lobby near the staircase ready to greet them and send them to Savannah Hall, the intimate room she'd reserved for the evening.

"Anne, how lovely to see you." Courtney air-kissed the Caucasian woman whom she'd met at another charity event.

"Thank you and welcome," Anne replied. "I'm so happy you could come to support the cause and take a look at my jewelry. I may not be on the board of directors any longer, but I am a survivor of domestic violence, so this organization is very near and dear to my heart."

"Well, I can't wait to see some of your pieces."

"And who is this gentleman behind you?" Anne inquired.

Courtney looked behind her at Jasper, who was trying to appear incognito. "Oh, him." She grabbed his arm and pulled him forward toward Anne. "This is Jasper Jackson."

Jasper held out his hand and Courtney watched the woman blush several shades of red. "A pleasure," Anne said softly.

"Likewise." Jasper's voice sounded husky even to Courtney, so she knew that Anne would be positively taken with him.

"Is it hot in here to you?" Anne asked, fanning herself.

Courtney smiled knowingly. Jasper's dark eyes on her or any woman had that effect. "There are quite a few people in the foyer." She helped the poor woman out. "Have my parents arrived?"

"Oh, yes. They're already upstairs."

"Thank you, I think we'll go find them," Courtney said, moving away. She met up with her parents and siblings, who were inside drinking champagne and admiring several pieces of jewelry. "Can anyone join this party?"

"Courtney, darling." Her mother came and kissed her cheek. "Where have you been? We were starting to get worried you wouldn't make it."

She blushed. They'd had a slight delay because of Jasper joining her in the shower, so it had taken longer than usual for her to get dressed. "Yeah, well…time got away from me."

She noticed Gabby snickering behind Shane. Clearly, her soon-to-be sister-in-law suspected she was lying.

"I saw a great piece that you must see," Kayla said, pulling Courtney away from Jasper.

"I'll join you." Gabrielle quickly joined the duo.

"You both look great," Courtney said once the trio was alone.

Kayla's dark curls hung beautifully over her white Grecian one-shoulder gown with beaded embellishments, while Gabby had definitely emerged from her former shell. She was wearing a blue strapless gown that hugged her body before fishtailing out like a mermaid.

"Yeah, yeah," Kayla said. "We know the reason you were late. It was written all over your face."

"Was I that transparent?" Courtney turned scarlet.

Gabrielle laughed. "Totally!"

Courtney joined in their laughter. "C'mon, you guys know how it is when a relationship is new. You can't get enough of each other."

"I hear you, girl," Gabrielle said. "Shane and I are like randy teenagers."

"And Ethan, well…" Kayla paused for effect. "I'll just say…he's very much an alpha male."

"Enough said," Courtney said. "Let's look at some of this jewelry."

Several displays were strategically set up throughout the ballroom. The ladies perused the displays noting which pieces they liked so their respective partners could buy them. Courtney eyed some sunflower diamond earrings for her mother and a diamond tassel necklace for herself.

She was behind a display case when she heard a female whisper, "Did you hear? That gorgeous gentleman in the black tuxedo is Andrew Jackson's son."

"Say it isn't so." The other female sounded shocked. "Isn't there a long-standing feud between the Adamses and Jacksons?"

"What do you mean?"

"The two families hate each other," the woman explained. "Jax Cosmetics is always trying to upstage media darling Adams Cosmetics. Thanks to that Adams girl, they are always in the paper. Have you seen her? She's absolutely stunning with those green eyes. No wonder the Jackson boy fell for her."

"I wonder what's going to happen. I can't imagine any good can come out of that union."

"I only hope Andrew doesn't show up tonight. You know his wife is good friends with Anne Burke." Were those women right? Was she fooling herself thinking that a relationship with her and Jasper could survive the strain?

Sure, she'd stood up to Andrew and told him to back off, but that didn't mean anything. He'd vowed that he would come between them. He would not allow an Adams to take another thing from him. His words had chilled her to the bone, and she hadn't forgotten them. And her father, well, Courtney doubted if he would ever come to accept Jasper in her life. Were they at an impasse?

"See something you like?" Jasper asked from behind her. Startled, Courtney spun around. Had he heard what those gossips had said?

He was smiling back at her, so clearly he hadn't. Perhaps she was making too much of the women's comments. Nothing had shown her that she and Jasper shouldn't be together. So why was there a sense of foreboding washing over her?

"What's wrong?" Jasper asked at the concerned look on Courtney's face. "Does someone have their eye on a piece you want?"

"It's nothing." Courtney shook her head and leaned across to give Jasper a hug.

"What was that for?"

She shrugged. "I don't know. I guess I just needed it."

"Well, whenever you need one, I'm here. C'mon, they're passing out some hot hors d'oeuvres in the main room and I'm starved."

"Sounds great." Courtney followed behind him.

Given her apprehension, their evening went surprisingly well. She watched her parents make small talk with Jasper, and Kayla and Gabby discuss Gabby's upcoming nuptials and bachelorette party, but despite the positive outcome she felt disaster was looming. It was as if she was waiting for the other shoe to drop.

Shane eventually pulled her aside and said, "Is everything okay, sis? You seem a little off tonight. You're not your usual sparkly self."

Courtney feigned a smile. "I'm sorry."

"Care to tell your big brother about it?"

Courtney peered from around his shoulder and glanced at Jasper. "Yes, but not here, okay?"

"How about outside?" Shane suggested. "I could use a little fresh night air." When they went out onto the terrace and into the spring air, Courtney shivered slightly. Shane removed his tuxedo jacket and wrapped it around her bare arms. "Better?"

Courtney nodded.

"So, why don't you tell me what has you so rattled?" he asked.

"I heard some gossip tonight and it kind of shook me."

"What did you hear?"

"It's nothing."

"C'mon, just tell me," Shane said.

"I was eavesdropping and heard some women gossiping earlier. They said no good would come of me and Jasper's relationship."

"And that bothered you?" Shane laughed. "You've been

dealing with a lot tougher critics, like Dad and Kayla, and you haven't faltered once. What's changed now? What aren't you telling me?"

Courtney turned away and looked out at the dark skies.

"What's going on, Courtney?"

She could hear the concern in Shane's voice and slowly turned around to face him. His piercing green eyes mirrored her own and she found it impossible to lie. "It's Andrew Jackson."

Shane's brow furrowed. "What about him?"

"After the dinner when I introduced Jasper to the family and Andrew interrupted...well, I went after him and confronted him," Courtney said. "That's when Andrew warned me that he'd had enough of Adamses taking what was his. He told me he would make me pay for taking his son away from him."

"He threatened you?" Shane looked as if he might pop a blood vessel. "How dare that bastard threaten my sister?"

"I think he was trying to scare me away." Courtney tried to defuse her brother's reaction. "I don't really think he meant me any harm." But even as she said the words, Courtney knew they were a lie. If Andrew Jackson had his choice, she and her entire family would be toast.

"I don't care," Shane said, pacing the terrace. "That man is a menace. First he attempted to blackmail Gabby and now he's threatening you. And I've had it up to here with him." He raised his hand above his head. "He's done nothing but try to hurt our family."

"And I think my relationship with Jasper has only made his animosity toward us even greater." Courtney sighed wearily.

"I'll handle this," Shane said, heading toward the door.

"Shane, please." Courtney grabbed his arm. "Please don't do anything rash. You're supposed to marry Gabby, the love of your life. Don't do anything that might jeopardize that." She wouldn't be able to bear it if something happened to him because of her.

He smiled and used his index finger to cross his heart. "Okay, okay, but we have to find a way to neutralize Andrew."

"Agreed."

Hours later, Jasper stood with Courtney outside the hotel, waiting for the valet to bring the Maserati around. Courtney was wearing the diamond tassel necklace and had the sunflower earrings in hand for her mother's birthday. Ethan and Kayla had left moments ago, and her parents and Shane and Gabby were wrapping up their purchases inside.

The paparazzi were across the street, snapping pictures of all the Atlanta socialites as they began to mill out of the hotel. "Courtney! Courtney! Courtney!" several of them yelled.

Courtney knew her part and walked toward the curb, posed so they could get another photo of her with her new jewelry and blew them a kiss. Jasper knew that any exposure she could get for Adams Cosmetics was worth the inconvenience of disrupting their evening.

"How about a picture with your new beau?"

It had not been lost on them that she'd been holding hands with Jasper when she'd walked in. She turned and batted her eyes at Jasper. "Do you mind?"

Jasper sucked in a breath. He hated the press, but he supposed this was part of the gig until Courtney was no longer the AC spokesmodel. But before he could get the word "okay" out of his mouth, he saw a man walking toward Courtney.

There was something about the man that looked suspicious. He was wearing dark clothes and a baseball hat.

He was covering his face with his jacket so it was hidden. The man was just a few feet away from Courtney now, and she hadn't noticed him approach. Seconds later, the man pushed Courtney off the curb. Courtney stumbled onto the street in the midst of oncoming traffic. She struggled to gain her balance.

Jasper had only seconds to react. He ran as fast as he could and pushed Courtney out of the way. She went flying across the pavement just as Jasper's body connected with the oncoming SUV and everything faded to black.

Chapter 16

"I'm okay," Jasper said, attempting to sit up in the hospital bed with little success. He was still a little woozy. Courtney was at his bedside in the E.R. in her dirty and torn sequined dress, fussing over him. She hadn't left his side since the moment he'd been taken by ambulance to the hospital. He'd been semiconscious during the ride, but he'd heard her crying and saying, "Stay with me."

"You're not okay." Courtney sighed. How could he be? He had lacerations on his face, a broken arm and several broken ribs and a slight concussion, but it could have been a lot worse. And since then, he'd been acting all manly and refusing to take pain meds. "I want to be in control of my faculties," he'd told the nurses.

"You could have died out there," Courtney said.

"But it would have been worth it," he said, touching her cheek. "If it would have saved you, then it would have been worth it." He leaned over and brushed his lips firmly over hers. When he pulled away, he noticed tears had formed in her eyes.

"Don't talk like that. If…if something had happened to you…" Courtney tried to hold her tears in check. She didn't want Jasper to know just how shaken she'd been or he would worry about her, when he was the one who'd been hurt. "I don't know what I would have done."

Everything had happened so quickly; she couldn't remember much except hitting the pavement, but when she'd looked up and seen Jasper lying in the street, not moving, her heart had stopped.

Using his good arm, Jasper stroked her honey-blond hair. "Same here. When I saw you in the street, all I could think about was that I had to get to you. I prayed that I would get to you in time."

"And thank God you did," Byron Adams said, holding the curtain open. Her mother was standing behind him, as was Shane, Gabby, Ethan and Kayla. Byron walked forward and the rest of the clan filed in behind him into the small, cramped quarters. "If it wasn't for your quick thinking, if you hadn't pushed my daughter out of the way, she could have been…" Her father's voice caught and her mother touched his arm. "Sh…she could have been killed tonight."

"I'm just glad I was there," Jasper said honestly.

"So am I." Once her father was in front of Jasper's bed, he held out his hand. "With no thought for yourself, you risked your life for my baby girl, and I just want to thank you."

Jasper stared in disbelief at Byron's outstretched hand, but he shook it anyway. "I would do it all over again."

A smile formed on her father's mouth. "I've no doubt you would."

"Dad's right," Kayla said, coming to the other side

of Jasper's bed so she could touch Courtney's shoulder. "You're a hero for what you did tonight."

"Yeah, it was pretty incredible," Ethan said as he joined Kayla and gave Courtney's shoulder a quick squeeze. "And you're one lucky man. I hear you only have a broken arm and some ribs."

"Don't go pinning any medals on me just yet," Jasper said. "I did what any one of you would have done for someone you love."

The room became silent and Courtney held her breath. Had she heard Jasper correctly? Had he just said he loved her in front of her entire family? She turned to look at him, and his eyes told her that there was much that needed to be said between the two of them, but now didn't seem like the right time.

The statement obviously caught her father by surprise because he immediately changed the subject. "Uh…well, what I want to know is how this happened. From the eyewitness accounts I've heard, it was like Courtney was deliberately pushed."

"But who would do something like that?" her mother asked.

"I mean, a car just happened to be there at that exact moment to run Courtney over?" Shane commented, as he pushed his way forward to the bed. "Sounds very suspicious to me."

"So you think someone meant to hit Courtney with their car?" Jasper inquired, looking directly at Shane.

Shane glanced at Courtney, who hung her head low, then looked back at Jasper. "I can't say for sure, but it could be."

"Well, Courtney is in the public eye a lot," Kayla said, trying to think the situation through logically. "It could have been some crazed fan. You know celebrities get stalkers all the time."

"Have you had any weird emails or fan mail?" Gabrielle asked.

Courtney shook her head.

"How about threats?" Ethan offered.

Courtney was silent.

"Well?" her father asked. "Has anyone threatened you?"

Courtney really did not want to get into this with her entire family present. She glared at Shane for starting this conversation. "No, not exactly."

From his bed, Jasper reached out and grasped Courtney's hand, pulling her closer to him. "What does that mean?" He peered into her eyes. She hated when he focused those midnight eyes of his directly on her. She felt utterly powerless against them. "Courtney?"

"I kind of had a heated discussion with your father," she finally said.

She saw her father instantly tense at this information, which was what Courtney had feared. Knots began to form in her stomach. He would be ready to fly off the handle at the thought of Andrew saying something menacing to her, and she didn't want that to happen.

"What was said, Courtney?" Jasper tugged at her arm so that she would turn back to face him. "What did Andrew say to you?"

"At the dinner party to introduce you to the family, I told him to back off, to leave you alone, that you wanted nothing to do with him and that he should stop attacking my family. I warned him that we were a tight-knit bunch and nothing he could ever do would break us."

"Good for you!" Kayla said.

"I'm sure he probably laughed at you. Andrew likes nothing better than taking potshots at us," Ethan added.

"Far from it," Courtney said. "He blamed me for taking you away from him." She squeezed Jasper's hand. "Told me that we Adamses—" she twisted so she could look at her family "—had taken enough away from him."

"Can you believe that, Elizabeth?" her father asked. "He still blames me for taking you away from him. It amazes me just how long that man can hold a grudge."

"But that's not all he said, is it?" Jasper said, guessing that there was more she wasn't saying. He also noticed that Shane was watching Courtney intently, which meant she hadn't told them the entire story.

"What else did he say?" her mother asked. "I want to hear exactly how evil the man I once cared for has become."

Courtney sighed heavily. "He said that he would make me pay for turning Jasper against him."

"See?" Her father pointed to no one in particular. "That's a threat. Andrew threatened our daughter. Oh, he's gone and done it now!" Her father paced the floor of the tiny room, making the space feel smaller. Courtney felt as if the walls were closing in.

She fought for control of her voice in an attempt to defuse her father's volatile temper. "They were merely words, Daddy. That doesn't mean Andrew would *physically* harm me. He'll probably just come after Adams Cosmetics like he's always done."

"But that doesn't mean he didn't mean you bodily harm," Shane cautioned, coming to Courtney's side. "Who knows what he's capable off, sis? Losing his son is personal. It could make Andrew more dangerous than he's ever been."

"Shane has a point," Ethan said. "I think it would be prudent if we got you a bodyguard."

Courtney stood up. "That's ridiculous. You're all blowing this way out of proportion." She walked toward her family. "I think everyone just needs to calm down."

"Maybe, but maybe not." Kayla joined the fray. "But we can't take that risk, Courtney. What if something happened to you? We wouldn't be able to live with ourselves."

"We protect our own," Shane added.

"I for one want to know what we're going to do about Andrew," her father stated. His arms were folded across his chest. "That man has been a thorn in my side for over a quarter of a century, and I have had enough."

"I will deal with my father."

All eyes turned to Jasper, who'd been quiet while they were all having their say on what should or shouldn't be done about Andrew. They seemed to have momentarily forgotten that Jasper was not only the one who was injured, but the one with whom Andrew was fixated.

"Jasper." Courtney rushed back to his side. "*I* would never ask you to do anything against your father."

"You're not asking," he responded. "I'm telling you." With some difficulty because of a bad arm, he pushed the pillows on the hospital bed back so he could sit up straight. "I will not allow my father to bully the woman I love."

There, he said it again. There was no mistaking his intent. He meant the words.

"I will find out exactly what my father is up to and put an end to this vendetta once and for all."

"That could be dangerous," Shane said.

"My father would never hurt me," Jasper said. It was the one thing he was absolutely sure of, despite Andrew's posturing that if Jasper wasn't with him, he was against him. Monica would and *could* never be his son. Jasper would have to play on Andrew's weakness and get him to admit his wrongdoings and get it on tape just as he'd done when he was fifteen. Except this time, Jasper wouldn't just be threatening to use the tape. This time he would expose Andrew for the lying, cheating sleazeball he truly was. It was the only way he and the Adams family would be free of him.

"He said he loves me," Courtney told Tea the following day when they met for coffee. She hadn't slept a wink the night before because images of the accident and Jasper lying in the street, and images of Andrew grabbing her by the arm and threatening her, haunted her. Not to mention, Jasper had said the L-word, and the anxiety about the discussion they'd yet to have had kept her up.

"And what did you say to him?" Tea asked, sipping on her white-chocolate mocha with whipped cream. She couldn't understand what all the fuss was about. If Courtney felt the way she suspected her best friend did, then his declaration of love should have been met with jubilation. So why did she see fear in Courtney's eyes?

"Say?" Courtney looked puzzled for a moment and motioned for Tea to wipe whipped cream from her upper lip. "Well, I couldn't say much of anything. My entire family was in the hospital room."

"Your family was in the room when he declared his love for the first time?"

"It was extremely awkward. It wasn't like we could have a discussion about it with my parents and siblings gathered around."

"So, what did you do?"

Courtney sipped her skinny cinnamon dolce latte. "I acted like I didn't hear him." When Tea raised her brow, she explained herself. "It wasn't the right time. Especially after I told them that Andrew verbally threatened me, the conversation escalated. I wanted to talk after my family finally left, but no sooner had I sat by his bedside than his mother came in, completely distraught. The rest of the evening before he drifted off to sleep was about convincing her that Jasper was going to be all right."

"Have you spoken with him today?"

Courtney shook her head. "I've been afraid to. I called the nurses' station and they said he was still sleeping."

"So you have some time to figure out how to approach the conversation."

"Exactly." Courtney pointed to her. "I mean, he did have a concussion and all. But, on the other hand, he did say it twice, that he 'saved the woman he loves.'"

"He said it twice? Sounds like he meant it."

"You really think so?"

Tea reached across the table and grasped Courtney's hand. "The bigger question here, Courtney, is whether you want it to be true. Do you love Jasper?"

Courtney's eyes swept over Tea's bronze face for a long moment and then tears slowly found their way down her cheeks. "I do. I love Jasper. The thought of losing him is too much to bear."

Tea leaned back, smiling with satisfaction. She'd known for a long time that Courtney was in love with Jasper, but it was nice to hear her best friend admit it. "Glad you're finally able to say it."

Courtney ran her fingers through her short crop of hair. "Near-death experiences can make you see things more clearly."

"Speaking of the accident," Tea said as she took a pinch of the blueberry muffin that Courtney had ordered but hadn't touched. "Do you really think someone meant to harm you?"

Courtney leaned forward in her chair and whispered, so no one could hear them, "You mean Andrew?" She suppressed a sigh. "I'm not sure. My family, Jasper, they all think he's capable, but sabotage has always been Andrew's style. He's never done anything this drastic before."

"He's never lost a son before."

"But he'd already lost Jasper," Courtney responded. "Jasper hasn't been a part of his life since he was a teenager."

"Which is why it was probably easy for Andrew to think he would get a second chance, but once Jasper made it clear that was no longer a possibility, he might have lost it." She snapped her fingers. "People do crazy things in the name of love."

"But how far would Andrew go to get *me* out of Jasper's life and back under his control?"

"That's the question of the hour."

Chapter 17

"I don't think you should do this," Abigail Jackson told Jasper at the hospital. He'd requested to be moved to the ICU to help with his plan. "Not only is Andrew dangerous when crossed, but what if he finds out what we're up to?" She'd been uneasy about calling Andrew and telling him Jasper had been hurt last night, but Jasper had been insistent.

"This is the only way, Mama. Andrew needs to know I've been seriously injured instead of Courtney. If he thinks I'm worse off than I am, it'll set the stage for me to get the truth out of him."

His mother sighed heavily. He knew she was against this, but this was his best defense. She hadn't left his side since last night, and as much as he wanted her to take care of him, she was going to mother him to death. She'd already fluffed his pillows half a dozen times. "Enough, Mama," he said. "They are fluffy enough."

Reluctantly, she sat down and watched him. She knew him well enough to know he was scheming. And she was right. He had business to take care of, namely putting a nail in Andrew's coffin. Nothing was going to give him greater pleasure than to stick it to the old man and catch him red-handed. His father had always covered his tracks well with his underhanded dealings. Only once had he been upstaged and that was when Jasper had overheard and taped a conversation with one of his lackeys and had gained the upper hand to secure his departure from Jackson Manor to live with his mother. Now lightning just needed to strike twice.

In the hospital, he'd had time to hatch his plan. He would wear a wire and get Andrew to admit the truth. He knew him well enough to know that if he believed Jasper was gravely injured, he might reveal his scheme to get rid of Courtney out of guilt. Then Jasper would have him right where he wanted him and could turn him into the authorities. Some might consider him heartless for what he was about to do, but Andrew had gone too far this time. He'd hurt Courtney, the woman Jasper loved.

And yes, he did love her. Love had sneaked up on him. He sure hadn't been planning or looking for it. But she'd had his heart from the moment she broke down on the side of the road in Punta Cana. Now that he knew, he wanted to shout his feelings from the rooftop and had just about done that last night with her entire family in the room.

He knew Courtney had heard him, but given the situation, they hadn't been able to have a private conversation. He was eager to hear her feelings. Could she love him as much he did her? He hoped so, because he knew with absolute certainty that she was the woman for him. He wanted to marry her.

Her family's blessing didn't seem as though it would be

hard to come by anymore. The fact that Byron had come to his hospital room to thank him for saving his daughter told Jasper that it might be possible after all. Of course, he didn't have a ring yet, but he would. He just had to deal with Andrew first.

His mother's voice jolted him out of his reverie. "Please tell me you will not do something stupid."

Jasper could feel her fear from the bed. "Mama, I won't take any unnecessary risks, but even you must see that this plan is brilliant."

She nodded. "I realize he might feel guilty if he thought he hurt you and this could open a window."

"That I could use to my advantage."

"I still don't like it."

"So you're okay!" Courtney said from the doorway.

When she'd gone to the hospital to visit him, she'd been shocked to find an empty bed. Her mind had immediately rushed to the worst possible conclusion. Did he have some sort of brain bleed they hadn't caught last night? She'd rushed to the nurses' station for details on Jasper's condition only to discover he'd been moved to ICU. Stone-cold fear had flooded through her. Why had no one called? When she felt inside her designer purse for her cell phone, she'd seen that it was off. Dead. In the midst of the ruckus from last night, she'd forgotten to charge it.

All Courtney could think about as she rode the elevator up to the eighth floor was that the doctor had been wrong last night and Jasper had been hurt trying to save her. If he died, she would never be able to live with the guilt. But when she arrived, she'd been shaking with joy and relief at seeing his handsome form sitting up in the bed looking healthy and strong.

Courtney quickly walked forward and hurled herself

into Jasper's arms. "You scared me half to death!" She lightly hit him on his good arm.

"It's okay, baby," Jasper crooned in her ear.

"When I didn't see you in your room, I freaked out," she said against his chest.

"I'm sorry about that. I did leave a message on your cell phone, but it went straight to voice mail."

Courtney inhaled Jasper's strong masculine scent. She was home. She looked up at him and couldn't resist stealing a kiss. She drew his face to hers, meaning the kiss to be light and quick, but his lips were warm and moist and when he deepened the kiss, he roused her passion.

"Uh…" Abigail coughed from behind them. "I…I'll just give the two of you some time alone." She quickly scuttled out of the room to give the lovebirds some privacy.

Courtney barely noticed her leave because she was so transfixed on the feel of Jasper's mouth on hers, strong and hard, and on the taste of his tongue. It was sweet as if he'd been nibbling on some cookies. When she finally lifted her head, she noticed a cup of tea and biscuits sitting on his nightstand.

"Wow, you must have really needed that," Jasper said, smiling broadly at Courtney's welcome.

She brought her hand up to her mouth to stifle a giggle. "I think I embarrassed your mother."

Jasper glanced at the doorway. "Oh, she'll be fine."

Courtney touched his cheek. "You're looking much better today, if not a little tattered and bruised." She fingered a scar above his brow and the black-and-blue marks on his face.

"Yeah, it takes a lot to keep me down."

"So, why did they move you to ICU?" Courtney asked.

"I spoke with the police and hospital administrator and I have a plan to address the Andrew situation. They agreed to help set up this sting in the hopes that my father will confess."

Courtney jumped up. "Jasper, there will be time for that later. Your health is more important than catching Andrew."

Jasper shook his head fervently. "I beg to differ. Now is exactly the time, because trust me, if Andrew felt like the job didn't get done the first time, he will try again. And he will be kicking himself that I got hurt."

Courtney shuddered. "You think he would send someone to come after me again?" The thought sent cold shivers up and down her spine.

"It's possible," Jasper answered honestly. "And I don't want to take that chance. I need to cut him off at the knees."

"I just don't want anything to happen to you," she cried, returning to the bed and the safety of his arms. "I couldn't bear it."

Jasper stroked her cheek. "I know. And don't think I don't know that we're overdue for a conversation when this is all over."

She smiled knowingly. He clearly hadn't been too groggy to remember he'd said he loved her.

"But I don't want any distractions when we talk," Jasper continued. "I just want it to be about you and me. No family. No feuds. Just us."

"I agree." And when the time came, Courtney wouldn't be afraid. Somehow she would find the courage to finally say the three words she'd never said to another man: I love you.

"How is Jasper doing?" her father asked when Courtney returned home later that evening. Jasper had requested she stay away, as he was sure Andrew would come to the hospital later that evening. She hated to leave him, but Jasper had insisted and told her the police would be nearby.

She was surprised to find the entire family assembled in the drawing room having cocktails. Kayla and Ethan were snuggled on a love seat, playing with Alexander. Shane and Gabby were standing in the corner kissing while her mother sat in a nearby chair. They all seemed surprised to see her.

Kayla inquired, "How's Jasper?"

"He's doing well, thanks," she said, taking a seat next to her on the couch.

"We didn't expect you tonight," her mother said. "We assumed you would be staying with Jasper in the hospital."

"Ummm..." Courtney replied, "his mother's with him, so I didn't want to intrude." Jasper had asked her not to reveal his plan to her parents until he had something concrete to tell them.

"I'm sure she appreciated that." Her mother reached across and patted Courtney's thigh.

"Well, I have to say that's a brave young man," her father said, straightening from the mantel he was leaning against. "Not many men would have stepped in the way of an oncoming car."

Courtney's face broke into an open smile. "Does that mean that you've changed your opinion about Jasper?"

Her father was silent for a moment and then he said, "I may have misjudged the young man. Clearly he's nothing like his father." A smile ruffled the corners of his mouth.

"Glad to hear that, Daddy." Courtney rose and walked over to give him a gentle squeeze. When she did, her father returned the hug. It had been tough being at odds with him over Jasper. She hadn't liked it one bit, so she was happy they were finding some common ground. Her father kissed her forehead the way he used to.

"Ah, peace and harmony in the family," her mother commented from the chair. "That's what I like to see."

"Almost, Mama," Shane said. "We still have the matter of Andrew to deal with."

"Why do we have to?" Gabrielle said. "Can't we just let it go? Perhaps the incident was an accident after all. We don't know for sure that Andrew sent someone after you."

"Do you forget what he did to you?" Shane asked.

Gabrielle turned to glare at her fiancé. "Blackmail and attempted murder are on total opposite ends of the spectrum. I'm just saying that we shouldn't rush to judgment." When Gabrielle said the words, Courtney noticed she looked directly at Byron.

"There's only one way to find out," Ethan said. "Jasper's going to have to talk to Andrew."

"Do you think Andrew would say anything incriminating?" Kayla wondered aloud. "He's been so clever in the past, with Noelle, the leak, the thefts. I don't know…"

"I guess that will depend on how good of an actor Jasper is," Shane said.

"But what if it backfires and Andrew is onto Jasper?" Courtney asked. Jasper had already set the plan in motion and there was no turning back.

"I think Andrew is desperate enough to have his son back in the fold that he won't realize he's being set up," her mother said.

"True," Ethan said. "Or Andrew may need a little incentive to believe Jasper has suddenly changed his mind."

"What are you thinking, Ethan?" Kayla asked.

"That we give Andrew a fake tip," Ethan said, "about an upcoming product. He'll be more likely to believe Jasper if he comes bearing gifts."

Byron nodded. "That's a brilliant strategy, Ethan." He

turned to Courtney. "When does Jasper go to see Andrew?"

"Soon," Courtney fibbed. She just prayed that when all was said and done, Jasper was standing and victorious in the end. And that Andrew would be out of their lives for good.

Chapter 18

"Abigail." Andrew nodded at her when he arrived at the ICU later that evening. She was sitting in a chair next to the bed where Jasper's still, motionless body lay. When she'd called Andrew that afternoon, he'd been shocked to hear her voice since he hadn't spoken to her in years. But that didn't matter because the moment she told him Jasper had been injured in a car accident, his heart had stopped.

Jasper? That couldn't be right. He'd set it in motion for Courtney Adams to have an accident. With her out of the way, whispering in his son's ear, he could finally get through to Jasper. He wanted his son back. He hadn't wanted him hurt.

Andrew walked forward into the room, his towering presence filling the tiny quarters. Jasper was hooked up to a lot of machines, and his face was battered and bruised. Had he done this? Had he done this to his own son? "How bad is it?" he asked, tears filling his eyes as he looked at his ex-wife.

"He sustained a severe blow to the head and ruptured his spleen. He had surgery late last night to repair some of the damage, but the swelling in his brain..." Abigail paused for effect and then reached for her handkerchief in her lap. "He...he hasn't woken up."

"Dear God!" Andrew's knees gave out and he sank to the floor, grasping hold of the bars on the hospital bed. "This can't be happening."

Abigail delivered the final blow. "And if he doesn't come out of in the next twenty-four hours..."

Andrew looked up at Abigail. "He will absolutely come through this. Our son is a fighter, Abigail. He's strong and resilient, like me. He will come through this."

Abigail didn't know if he was saying it more for her or himself. She rose from the chair. "I'm going to get some coffee. Would you like some?"

Andrew shook his head. "No. But thank you for the time alone with him."

Abigail patted Andrew's shoulder on her way out.

"I'm so sorry, son," Andrew whispered, leaning down to stroke Jasper's forehead. "This wasn't supposed to happen. *You* weren't supposed to be here." He rose to his feet. "Damn those Adamses. They must have some guardian angel. Every time I try... How did she escape that car? And why were you there?"

Andrew paced the floor of the room. "I don't understand this. But you can rest assured that I will take care of this, son. Once and for all. I will finish those Adamses if it's the last thing I do. It's their fault you're in this bed, and they will pay."

That threat caused Jasper to open his eyes and Andrew looked down at him. "Son!" He bent over and hugged Jasper. "Thank God!" He rushed out of the room to the nurses' station. "Call the doctor. My son is awake." He quickly walked back to the room. "I'm so happy to see you awake."

"Dad?" Jasper croaked. He knew calling him "dad" would tug at Andrew's heartstrings because he hadn't called him that in years. "Where...where am I?"

"You're in the hospital," Andrew said softly. "You were in a car accident, but you'll be all better before you know it. I promise you."

A doctor and several nurses came inside the room, ushering Andrew out of the room and into the hallway. "We need to examine him."

Jasper could see Andrew staring at him through the glass window of the ICU room.

"Don't worry, son," he heard his father say on the way out. "I'm here for you. I'm here for you always."

"It's not enough," the police detective told Jasper and Abigail when they came into the room after Andrew had gone.

"What do you mean?" Jasper said. "He all but admitted that he tried to hurt Courtney."

"I agree with my son," his mother stated. "Andrew is dangerous."

"It's still not enough," the detective said. "We certainly have reason to suspect Mr. Jackson is behind the accident, but that's all we have. We have no evidence of payoff, we don't have the driver of the car and he didn't fully admit to you that he'd done it."

"What else is it going to take?" Courtney said from the doorway. She'd waited as long as she could at the estate, and now she couldn't wait any longer. She'd had to know what was happening, so she'd driven back to the hospital.

"Does Andrew have to make another attempt on my life before you *do* something?"

"Not at all, Ms. Adams," the detective said. "Your safety is our utmost concern. We can put a tail on you to ensure that you're looked after."

"For how long?" Jasper said. "Because trust me, my father won't stop coming after them."

"Then get me proof," the detective responded, "something I can take to the D.A. to make a case."

"Fine!" Jasper said. "I'll get you your proof."

"Are you okay?" Kayla asked Courtney several days later when she found her staring out of her office window. "You look so far away."

Courtney turned around. "Just thinking."

"It has been a pretty dramatic week," Kayla said.

"It has been." Courtney nodded. She hadn't felt much like coming into work after what had gone down with Jasper and his father, but she did have a job to do.

"Is there anything I can do?" Kayla asked.

"No, there's nothing anyone can do," Courtney said. "Andrew Jackson has it out for me and hired a hit man to come after me." After hearing what Andrew had told Jasper when he thought he was unconscious, she was sure he'd intended to hurt her. "I have a police escort because I'm afraid of what he'll do next. And the man I love is going to the lion's den to try and get the goods on his father. No, I don't think you can help with this one, big sis."

"I'm so sorry," Kayla said. Courtney could hear the sorrow in her voice. "I don't know how this all spun so far out of control. Please, come sit with me." She held out her hand and Courtney reluctantly walked toward her and grasped it. They walked over to the couch in her office and sat down.

"I'm not holding up too well, am I?"

"How can you?" Kayla said softly. "You don't know when the other shoe is going to drop."

"I'm scared," Courtney said, "not only for myself, but for Jasper. His father is a man bent on revenge. He doesn't strike me as a forgiving person. If he finds out Jasper is onto him and tried to set him up, he might finally lose all his marbles."

Kayla laughed. "True, but this family takes care of our own. We will not let anyone harm you or Jasper."

"Kayla's right," Shane said from the doorway of her office. "Did you forget we're the three musketeers?" He walked toward the duo with his hand outstretched. "One for all…"

"You do realize how corny this is, right?" Kayla said, her eyes smiling at Shane as she too held out her hand.

"But effective," Courtney said, and held out her hand. "And all for one." The three siblings joined in a group hug.

Jasper shuddered as he drove his Maserati into the gates of Jackson Manor. When he'd left when he was fifteen years old, he'd vowed to never return. But now he was back, and it left a sour taste in his mouth. He'd been released from the hospital a few days ago. With both Courtney and his mother hovering and making sure he rested, he'd had plenty of time to figure out how best to approach Andrew. Jasper knew he had to convince Andrew that he was willing to try at a father-son relationship. What better way than to come to the enemy's court?

The manor looked every bit as daunting as it had when he'd been a child. There wasn't a single warm moment that Jasper could reach back into his memory to grasp. As soon as his mother had left when he was seven, it had been hell on earth. One nanny after another, then boarding school with other entitled students with wealthy parents.

When he rang the bell, an imposing-looking man in a black coat, who Jasper assumed was the butler, answered the door.

"May I help you?" he asked with a booming voice. It seemed to echo in the whitewashed foyer. The old dark wooden staircase was gone, and in its place was a stark marble one.

"I'm here to see my father."

"Excuse me?" The man seemed confused. Clearly, he didn't know Andrew had a son.

"I'm Jasper Jackson," he said. "Andrew's son."

"My apologies." The butler lowered his head. "I will let Mr. Jackson know you are here. Let me show you to the drawing room."

"I would appreciate that," Jasper said, looking around. Much had changed since he'd last been in the house. The interior was not nearly as intimidating as the outside. Must have been Blythe Jackson's touch. The interior was all white walls, cream carpet and various African artifacts and paintings on the walls.

The butler led Jasper down the hall to a large, airy room and then closed the door behind him as he went to fetch Andrew.

Jasper noticed a Monet and a Renoir on the wall. Whether they were originals or prints, Jasper didn't know or care, but he suspected Blythe did. She probably wanted everyone to know that she knew a little something about artwork. He went to the mantel and there were pictures of Andrew, Blythe and Monica, both together and apart. *One happy family,* thought Jasper.

He didn't hear the door open and close behind him, but suddenly he heard a cold, feminine voice. "And what the hell do you think you're doing here?" Monica asked.

Jasper spun around to face the she-devil. She was wearing a scowl to go along with the black riding coat, breeches and riding boots she had on. She was holding a leather riding crop and was hitting it against her hand. He'd bet she wanted to use the crop to smack him across the head. "Why, Monica, what a pleasure to see you again," he said, sarcasm dripping from his voice.

"I'll ask you again," she said, walking forward. "What the hell are you doing here?" She surveyed him, taking in the cuts and bruises on his face. "And what the hell happened to you?"

"Car accident."

"Hmm…I wonder who suffered more damage, you or the car." She laughed to herself. "But you still haven't answered my question. And since you didn't, let me give you a piece of advice. There's no place for you here."

Jasper smiled smugly because he knew the exact opposite to be true. Andrew would jump at the chance to have him back and throw this wannabe so far she wouldn't be able to blink. "Is that right?"

"Yes, that's right." She hated his smugness and started circling around him. "Andrew and I have been running Jax Cosmetics for years. And we don't need you."

"Thanks for taking care of my inheritance," Jasper said. He could see she was on the edge and enjoyed baiting her.

Monica's eyes glowed fire. "Andrew promised me that he would leave everything to me. And I know he will. He will see all the hard work I've put in and reward me accordingly. He will not let *you* come in and take what belongs to me."

Jasper bent down until he was facing Monica eye-to-eye. "It was never yours to begin with. *I* was born a Jackson. Your mother just married one." He could see Monica was about to slap him and quickly sidestepped her blow.

"Now, now," Andrew said from the doorway. "Let's all get along."

"He's miserable, Andrew," Monica said, rushing to his side and hugging his middle since she was only five-six to his six-six. "He said the most horrible things to me."

"And I'm sure you didn't provoke him, right, sweetheart?" he said, patting her on the head.

Monica seemed appalled by his comment. "Of course not, Daddy."

"Why don't you go on your ride with your mother? She's waiting in the stables and I need to talk to my son."

Jasper watched Monica bristle at the word "son." Clearly, she had thought their father-son relationship was over, so she was disappointed to hear otherwise. With her head lowered, she slowly walked toward the door. She gave Jasper one final withering glance before she departed.

When the door closed, Andrew walked over to Jasper and enveloped him in a large hug. Jasper pulled away quickly, since he didn't want Andrew to feel the wire he was wearing underneath his clothes. He'd met up with the police detective in an unmarked van up the road from the manor so he could be wired up. He was determined to get Andrew to talk. "I'm surprised, but happy to see you here, Jasper. It looks like you're healing well."

"I'm made of tough stock," Jasper responded evenly.

"Yes, you are." Andrew went over to a large wingback chair, sat and folded his arms across his chest. "But that still begs the question as to why you came. You know I love you and always will, but I thought you said you wanted nothing more to do with me. You said you would never come back to Jackson Manor."

"Near-death experiences have a way of making you re-evaluate things, and I realize I may have been too harsh on you."

Andrew snorted. "Ya think?"

Jasper sucked in his breath. "Well, I'm here now."

"And?"

"I was thinking that maybe we could try having some sort of relationship." Jasper sat down on the couch across from Andrew.

Andrew leaned forward in his chair and looked him square in the eye. "You know that's all I've ever wanted."

"Good, because it looks like things with me and Courtney have stalled. She's been distant since the accident."

"You mean the witch abandoned you during your time of need? After you saved her? What kind of woman does that?" Andrew had read the papers. Witnesses had said Jasper stepped in front of the SUV and pushed Courtney out of danger.

"I guess she was truly just looking for a fling and things have gotten too serious for her," Jasper said. "I think our affair may be over."

"But you don't want it to end, do you?" Andrew asked. He could recognize the signs of a man besotted with unrequited feelings. It was as if he were looking in a mirror at himself when he'd been spurned by Elizabeth.

Jasper nodded. Ah, he'd found the hook. He would tap into Andrew's history with Courtney's mother. "It's hard, you know, when you put yourself out there and your feelings aren't returned, makes me feel like I'm not good enough for her." He bowed his head in his hands and massaged his temples. He was trying hard to give the appearance of a man distraught. "I suppose it would never have worked anyway. Ever since that dinner you interrupted, the Adamses haven't trusted me. It's been an uphill battle ever since. She probably gave in to pressure to end our relationship."

"Apparently that's what the women in that family do,"

Andrew replied. "Toss you aside when they're done with you."

"Anyway…I think I might go back to Punta Cana," Jasper said, rising from the sofa. He walked over to the window and peered out, hoping the police were getting every word of their conversation. "Life there was simple, easier."

"You don't have to leave, son," Andrew said, coming up behind Jasper. Grasping his shoulders, he turned Jasper around. "You and I, we can get back at the Adamses. And you can stick it to that witch in the process."

"I don't know…"

"Don't you want to get back at her for how she's treated you?" Andrew said, egging him on. "Trust me, revenge would be sweet."

"I'm a hotelier. I know hotels. I don't know anything about the cosmetics business."

"Don't worry." Andrew wrapped his arm over Jasper's shoulders and walked him away from the window. "I can show you."

He moved over to a painting and pulled it down to reveal a safe underneath. "I have been sticking it to those Adamses for years." He moved the safe dial several times back and forth and then opened it. He removed some of its contents. "That—" he threw down a notebook "—is the formula to Ecstasy. We used it to re-create a fragrance for Noelle."

He threw down several photos. "That is the prototype to Ecstasy's bottle. We leaked it to the press. All thanks to Noelle Warner and James Burton. I couldn't have asked for a better cohort. She kind of fell into my lap thanks to Ethan Graham's arrogance. Of course, there's more from over the years, but I won't bore you. But with you on my side, who knows how much more damage we can inflict on them?"

Jasper couldn't believe Andrew was laying his darkest secrets bare, all because he wanted Jasper back in the fold. "And we can do more," Andrew continued. "All you have to do is cozy back up to that Adams girl, make sweet love to her and she'll tell you all her secrets. She struck me as not the brightest one in that bunch."

If only he knew. Courtney was just as smart as Kayla and Shane. "You've gone pretty far in to attack the Adams family, Dad. Just how far did you go?" Jasper asked.

He already had the evidence he needed to nail Andrew on corporate espionage, but he needed the goods on his attempt on Courtney's life.

Andrew looked up at him, disoriented. "What do you mean?"

Jasper's eyes turned cold as ice as he stared at the man that was his father. "How far did you go?" He watched Andrew draw in a deep breath as understanding dawned on him. He knew Jasper knew the truth. "Answer me!"

"Listen, son." Andrew took a step toward him, but Jasper stepped backward. "I don't know what you think you know, but you were never supposed to get hurt."

"What was supposed to happen?"

"The Adams girl was supposed to get hurt, not you. I hired someone to push her in the street and then a car would accidentally hit her. I just wanted her out of your life, and obviously she wants you out of hers too. Why else would she treat you so callously after you saved her life? I did it all because I wanted you back."

"And you would do anything to get me back here, in this house?" Jasper motioned to the room. "My God, do you even realize what you have done?"

"I...I love you, son," Andrew cried. Tears were falling from his eyes and he was visibly distraught, running his fingers through his slick black hair until it stuck up on his head. "I would never put you in harm's way, you must know that."

"What I know is that you tried to hurt the woman I love," Jasper returned. "And that's unforgivable."

"But I did it for you, for us," Andrew said, wiping the tears from his eyes, "to bring you back to the fold."

"Then you're delusional," Jasper replied, "because I don't need or want your kind of love, the kind of love that makes you willing to commit murder." He made for the door, but the police detective and several uniformed officers were already walking into the study.

Andrew looked at Jasper, blinking with bafflement. "What...what's going on?"

Jasper ripped open his button-down shirt to reveal the wire. "The police heard everything," he responded. "They heard how you've sabotaged the Adams family for years, but most important they have you on attempted murder."

"Jasper." Andrew pleaded with his eyes as one of the uniformed officers cuffed him and read him his rights. "How could you do this? You must know I never meant to harm you."

"You harm everything you touch," Jasper said.

"I'm sorry," Andrew said as the police officers led him toward the door. "I'm sorry I couldn't be the father you always wanted and needed, the father you deserved."

Just then Monica and Blythe came through the study doors. "What's going on here?" Monica asked, looking at the police and then back at Jasper. "What have you done?"

"More like what has Andrew done?" Jasper replied, walking up to her. He bent down and whispered so only she could hear him, "I don't know if you played a part in Andrew's scheme to kill my girlfriend, but my advice would be to get a good lawyer. Because all of this—" he motioned to the house "—may not be yours to inherit. Have a nice life."

Chapter 19

"We can't thank you enough for everything you've done, Jasper," Elizabeth Adams told him when he came to the Adams estate the next morning. He'd been at the police station giving his witness statement until late the day before and hadn't been able to update all the Adamses on his success. When the morning paper had been delivered, they'd all been shocked to see the headline Cosmetics Tycoon Andrew Jackson Arrested for Attempted Murder.

At the breakfast table, Shane had called Ethan and Kayla, who too were in stunned disbelief. They'd rushed over to the estate to find out from Courtney what had occurred. Now they were all gathered in the Adamses' living room, listening to the sordid tale of Andrew Jackson's crimes. Courtney and Jasper and her mother were seated on the sofa while Ethan and Kayla shared the love seat. Her father was standing by the mantel, his usual spot at family meetings.

"You did so at great personal risk to yourself," Elizabeth continued.

"Mom's right," Shane said. He and Gabby were standing by the terrace doors. "We owe you a debt of gratitude. We've been trying to take down Andrew for years and were unsuccessful."

"This…this is huge" was all Kayla could muster. As CEO, she'd been battling with Jax Cosmetics for years since her father handed the reins to her almost seven years ago. She was in disbelief that it was finally over.

"What I can't believe is that Andrew copped to everything he'd done," Shane said. "And I'm sure what he said on tape wasn't the half of it."

"The police are still going through the items in his safe," Jasper said, "so there will probably be more to come."

Elizabeth shook her head in dismay. "It amazes me the lengths Andrew went to hurt us. To hurt Courtney. It breaks my heart."

"Do you feel sorry for him, Mama?" Courtney asked.

"Of course not. It's just so hard to believe how far he strayed from the nice boy I once knew. I'm just thankful Jasper got him to admit what he'd done before he tried to hurt you again." Her eyes brimmed with tears when she looked at Courtney and Jasper.

"You don't owe me anything," Jasper said. "I did it for this one." He pulled Courtney toward him until she was snuggled securely in the crook of his arms. "But I also did it because it was the right thing to do."

"What do you think will happen to Jax Cosmetics?" Gabrielle wondered aloud.

"We cut off the head and I think the body will wither and die," Ethan replied, "because Monica, well, she's good, but she's not qualified enough to lead the company. Plus,

I suspect once the investigation is done, we'll find out she had a hand in some of Andrew's underhanded dealings."

"I've no doubt," Jasper said. "That woman is a barracuda."

"I'm just happy this is all behind us," Courtney said.

Her father, who'd been surprisingly quiet throughout the conversation, walked toward them. Jasper didn't know what to expect, so he was surprised when Byron offered his hand to him. When Jasper went to shake it, Byron pulled him up and into a hug. "Welcome to the family, son."

Cheers erupted in the room and Jasper saw that Courtney had to fight back the tears that were threatening to fall.

Jasper smiled broadly as he looked down at Courtney. It meant a great deal to him to earn Mr. Adams's respect. He wasn't an easy man to like, but he was a fair one and Jasper appreciated that. They had come a long way. "Thank you, sir." He hoped to be asking him for Courtney's hand in marriage very, very soon.

"Well, if you'll excuse us," Jasper said, grabbing Courtney's hand and pulling her out onto the terrace. "It's been one helluva week and we have a talk that's long overdue."

"You lovebirds have fun now." Gabrielle gave Courtney a wink as the couple opened the terrace doors and walked out into the cool morning air.

They walked hand in hand in silence for some time, neither saying a word. It had been a drama-filled few weeks. There had been lies, betrayal, revelations and confessions, but there was still one confession left to be made.

Courtney breathed in the scent of hibiscus and rose from her mother's garden until they came to a stone bench in the middle of the garden and sat down. Jasper turned to face Courtney. He stroked her cheek while gazing into her eyes.

"I'm glad we're finally alone," Jasper said.

"So am I."

"There's a lot I've wanted to say for a while now, but the timing hasn't been right. But it is now. And I want to tell you what's in my heart."

"Yes…?"

"The night of the accident," Jasper began, "put a lot of things into perspective for me. It made me see how close I came to losing you and it scared me. The only thing I can remember is seeing you falling into that street with oncoming traffic. The fear of losing you made me spring into action."

"You leaped in front of that car," Courtney said, her green eyes widening. "I'd never seen anything so daring, so crazy, so absolutely amazing in my entire life. I doubt most men would have done the same."

"All I knew was that I had to get to you. I didn't want to lose you without getting the chance to tell you how I feel."

"And how do you feel?" Courtney whispered tenderly.

"I love you, Courtney," Jasper said. "I know I said it a couple of times at the hospital, but I didn't get to tell you in private that I fell in love with you in Punta Cana. From the moment I saw those sexy shorts and long legs on the pavement, I was a goner. I enjoyed our time in and out of bed more than even I realized. It wasn't until you left without a word that I realized just how much you'd come to mean to me."

"My family needed me," Courtney said.

"I know, I know," Jasper murmured, but then Courtney interrupted him with a finger to his lips.

"You know that's not completely the truth." She had to stop lying to herself and to him. "I used my family's business as an excuse to come home. Our relationship was moving so fast, so quick, that it snuck up on me. I wasn't ready for it all, so when the opportunity presented itself, I ran."

"I understand fear." Jasper nodded. "Distance didn't get you out of my system, and I decided to follow you back here to Atlanta, desperate to find out why you left and make you regret leaving me. But little did I know that I would fall harder for you, that you would come to mean more to me than life itself. I love you, Courtney Adams."

"Jasper..."

"I know we've had a tough road to get here, with my lying to you about who I was, my father and all his attempts to hurt you and your family, and your family being against us, but that's all behind us now. You and me, we are unbreakable, so I'm hoping that you can see a future with me. A long future. Please tell me you do."

"I love you, Jasper," Courtney said. "I love you with all my heart."

"You do?" he said, hope springing up in his voice.

Courtney nodded. "I've known for some time, but like you I've been afraid and denied the feelings existed, but they've been there all along. You've done so much for me, for my family. My love for you is eternal and I see a long, happy future with you, Jasper Jackson."

"As Mrs. Jackson?"

"Is someone asking?"

He chuckled and then scooted off the concrete bench to kneel in front of her. "Courtney Adams, will you marry me?"

"Yes, I will marry you." Courtney wrapped her arms around him and kissed him with all the love that was in her heart. They fell back onto the grass with Jasper taking the full weight of her. A quiver of love and happiness flowed through her, because at last she'd found her home.

Epilogue

"To Courtney and Jasper!" Shane held up his wine flute.

"To Courtney and Jasper!" The Adams family held up their flutes to celebrate the newly married couple.

The entire Adams family and a few close friends like Tea, Mark and Piper had been invited to Courtney and Jasper's destination wedding at Sea Breeze Resorts in Punta Cana for Christmas later that year.

Jasper hadn't wanted a long engagement. He wanted Courtney as his wife as soon as possible. Soon after he'd proposed, he'd slid a beautiful ring with a center stone set with pavé diamonds on her finger and then started making wedding preparations. They'd agreed to a small, intimate gathering at the place where they fell in love. Mark stood up as his best man with Shane and Ethan as groomsmen while Tea was her maid of honor and Kayla and Gabby were her bridesmaids.

Courtney and Jasper turned to look at each other and he

leaned in for a kiss. When his lips met hers, her lips parted to release a sigh of pure delight. Courtney beamed with love at the man that was her friend, her partner, her lover for life. She couldn't wait for what the future had in store.

"Hello, Mrs. Jackson. Have I told you that you look absolutely radiant today?" he asked.

The strapless taffeta gown she wore with floral appliqués had a formfitting bodice and a cascading train. Her beautiful honey-blond hair was spun in delicate curls behind a simple headpiece and a cathedral-length veil.

"I believe you did, once or twice." She smiled with delight.

Just then, Courtney's father walked up to them.

"Can I steal a moment with the groom?" her father asked.

"Sure, Daddy." Courtney moved away to allow them to speak. It would give her a few minutes to congratulate her sister-in-law, Gabby, who'd revealed during the rehearsal dinner that she and Shane were expecting. They'd only been married four months. Her brother sure hadn't wasted any time.

"I don't need to tell you that I expect you to make my daughter very happy," Byron told Jasper.

"No, you do not, sir." Jasper shook his head. "Because I most certainly will spend the rest of my life treating your daughter like the princess she is."

Byron smiled broadly. "I know you will, son." He patted his shoulder affectionately. "You're a good man and my daughter is lucky to have you."

"I sure am," Courtney said, slipping her arm around her father's waist as she came back to join them. "Because I had a father like you who helped me realize what a great man is like."

"Th…thanks, baby girl."

Courtney could see her father was visibly moved and he nodded at her before stepping away.

"I think you almost made your dad cry," Jasper said in disbelief.

Courtney shrugged. "He needed to know that I found the man I love. Because forever is how long I'm going to love you, Jasper."

"Forever," Jasper murmured, kissing her to seal the promise.

* * * * *

KPAB4840912

REQUEST YOUR FREE BOOKS!

2 FREE NOVELS
PLUS 2 FREE GIFTS!

KIMANI ROMANCE™

Love's ultimate destination!

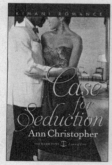
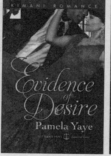
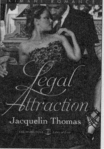

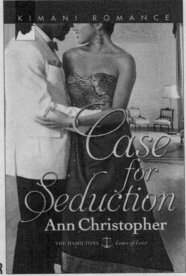